Lost Boy

Also by Linda Newbery

At the Firefly Gate

Set in Stone

Shell House

Sisterland

Lost Boy

LINDA NEWBERY

David Fickling Books

OXFORD · NEW YORK

A DAVID FICKLING BOOK

Published by David Fickling Books
an imprint of Random House Children's Books
a division of Random House, Inc.
New York

Originally published in Great Britain by Orion Children's Books, a division of
the Orion Publishing Group Ltd, in 2005.

DAVID FICKLING BOOKS and colophon are trademarks of David Fickling.

www.randomhouse.com/kids

Educators and librarians, for a variety of teaching tools, visit us at
www.randomhouse.com/teachers

Library of Congress Cataloging-in-Publication Data
Newbery, Linda.
Lost boy / Linda Newbery. — 1st American ed.
p. cm.
SUMMARY: After Matt moves to Hay-on-Wye in Wales, a boy his age
who bears the same initials and was killed in a car accident many
years earlier, appears to Matt.
ISBN 978-0-375-84574-1 (trade) — ISBN 978-0-375-93617-3 (lib. bdg.)
[1. Ghosts—Fiction. 2. Traffic accidents—Fiction. 3. Hay (Wales)—Fiction.
4. Wales—Fiction. 5. Mystery and detective stories.] I. Title.
PZ7.N4715Lo 2008
[Fic]—dc22
2007015041

Printed in the United States of America
10 9 8 7 6 5 4 3 2 1
First American Edition

for Bethan Hughes

Contents

ONE

M.L.

Everywhere was so *big* out here; that was what amazed him.

At first, Matt had expected it all to be little and cute: there'd be small villages, narrow streets and lanes, people spending their whole lives on farms or in cottages, half lost in the countryside. But now, out on his bike, pausing on the bend before the hedges closed in on the long swoop down to Hay, he was overwhelmed by bigness and space. The landscape – green, more shades of green, lush and alive and *greener* green than he'd known green could be – spread out like a map: no, like one of those dioramas he'd seen in museums, where a painted landscape stretched endlessly into distance. Here, the hills and woods and valleys reached out farther than his eyes could see: England in front and to the east, Wales behind him and west. He was beginning to recognize the nearest bits; but changes in light or weather could make everything look different, throwing bright patches of green-gold on to distant hills, or hiding the town in mist.

By now it was Milton Keynes, where he used to live, that seemed – well, if not small, at least *measurable*, and mapped, and familiar.

Matt felt himself fizzing with the joyful sense that only the beginning of school holidays can bring; and it wasn't even the first day yet, school having finished after lunchtime. Two whole weeks of freedom stretched ahead, and it felt like spring at last, and the evenings were light enough to stay out on his bike. At last, he could properly explore, and feel he lived here.

The lane was hardly more than a track, plunging downhill between tall hedges. Taking a deep breath, he pushed off; he felt the rush of air against his face and through his hair, and the irresistible whizz of speed that sang in his ears. Hedges and trees rushed back in a blur, the wind batted his lashes and gusted into his mouth, his knuckles were tight on the handle-bars. The bike was almost out of control in this headlong swoop – his reward for the tiring slog up. His eyes watered as he looked to the bend ahead. Here he'd have to brake, bring the giddy rush to an end, freewheeling on down the gentler slope that led to the main road.

The bend, and the solid trunk of a tree right on the corner, slammed into view faster than he could gather his wits. He heard no engine sound until the Land Rover was speeding towards him. Too late, he realised that it wasn't a bend, but a T-junction. He swerved violently to the right, braking hard, too hard, almost pitching himself over the handlebars. In an instant of panic he glimpsed a face behind the windscreen, hands on the wheel; heard the skid of tyres and the screech of brakes as the Land Rover loomed. It was inevitable: the second before the collision stretched out into long slowness. Then the impact of metal meeting metal jarred through him, and a floating sensation of being lifted right off the bike and dumped on the grass verge, sprawling on his side.

After a shocked moment, he registered that he was still alive. His eyes were open, staring at grass stems and ridgy tree bark, and he smelled the coolness of earth. The heavy fall had slammed the air out of his lungs; his first breath felt like surfacing from underwater. He tried moving a hand, then his whole arm.

One leg, then the other. Everything seemed to work. He pushed himself up and looked at the bike, flat on the empty road, one pedal still rotating.

The empty road.

Dizzy, he got to his feet.

No Land Rover, no driver: just him and his bike. But he'd heard no sound of a vehicle driving away; no one had shouted to him, asked if he was all right. He looked along the road in all directions, all three branches of the T. Nothing. No one. No smell of burning rubber, no tyre marks, no exhaust fumes.

How long had he been lying there? Only a minute, surely?

Sick and shaken, he was unable to make sense of what had happened. Had he only dreamed the Land Rover? But he hadn't dreamed coming off his bike. His left arm and thigh were bruised and sore; looking down, he saw grass stains on his jeans and sweatshirt, and some muddy smears. Nothing worse.

His bike was unmarked. No buckling or bending; not even any scrape marks on its paint. He righted it, checking that no spokes had been damaged. Then, pushing it to the verge, he came face to face with his own initials, on the trunk of the tree.

M.L.

Matthew Lanchester.

He did a real double-take: looked away and back, to check that he really had seen it.

Yes, he had. M.L., carved on a little wooden cross nailed into the tree trunk.

For a bewildering second, he thought he'd died after all, and was revisiting the place of his death. Either that or he was dreaming.

He looked again. Sometimes, on roadside verges, he'd seen brown shrivelled flowers pinned to a tree or a lamp post, the remnants of a florist's bouquet with tatters of ribbon, and knew that someone must have died there. 'Oh, how awful,' Mum would say, if they were in the car, and she'd give a sort of shudder, twitching away bad thoughts. For some reason, these tributes were often in the shape of an anchor. Maybe the friends, relatives, whoever they were, wanted to anchor the memory of the dead person to the place where they'd died. That was weird, Matt thought, because if you'd died horribly in an accident, what could be worse than being tethered for ever to the place where it happened?

The place of death. He wished that thought hadn't sneaked into his mind. It was so peculiar to stand looking at his own initials, carved on the cross. He had a feeling that time had come to a standstill, along with him and his bike. He could hear baa-ing – the deep voices of sheep and the higher, bleatier ones of lambs. Rooks cawed in the treetops. Behind these sounds was only the deep quiet of the evening.

There was no anchor here: just the plain, simple cross with the letters M.L. cut into it, fastened to the trunk with rusty nails. The tree was sturdy, with deeply-grooved, grey-brown bark. Although new leaves were opening all along the hedgerow, this tree was still twiggy and bare. His gaze dropped to the rough grass. There, propped against the base of the trunk, was a bunch of flowers: daffodils, some with pointed buds, others opened into frilled trumpets, their fat stems held with an elastic band. They looked fresh-picked. Someone had come here specially, Matt thought, for M.L. Today?

The cross, though, must have been here for some while. The nails holding it in place were rusty; the wood looked damp and weathered, with edges starting to crumble and flake. *That proves it can't be me,* Matt thought, impatient with himself for thinking something so daft. But someone remembered M.L., whoever M.L. was; someone cared enough to bring flowers.

He felt a prickling at the back of his neck, and the certainty that he was being watched; but – he checked all ways – there was no one in sight. His hands fumbled as he mounted the bike. Standing on the pedals, pressing down hard, he cycled off fast in the direction of Hay.

TWO

Wil

Hay-on-Wye was a town of books. All the tourist signs and leaflets said so, and it was impossible not to notice, as you walked or biked through the streets, that there were more bookshops than anything else. There were books in almost every window; stands and boxes of them spilled on to the pavements, lined the alleyways, and filled the castle courtyard. Not new books: to Matt, most of them looked like ancient, dull, dusty stuff no one could possibly want, but people came specially to Hay and spent whole days exploring the thirty-something bookshops. Mum said that almost any book you wanted, you'd find somewhere in Hay; or if it wasn't there now, it would turn up sooner or later. And as if there weren't enough bookshops already, she and Dad had opened one of their own.

Lanchesters was their dream. Dad had been made redundant, and soon afterwards Grandad had died, leaving his house in Aylesbury to be sold. Mum and Dad had decided to take the chance of a move and a new way of life. The money from two houses – theirs, and Grandad's bigger one – added up to enough to buy the house and shop in Lion Street. The Laurels, its name before they changed it, was a hundred and fifty years old. It was more than twice as big as the semi they'd had in Milton Keynes, and many times more interesting. It had an attic, where Matt and Fen, his sister, had their bedrooms; it had a cellar, and a shed in the garden that had once been a stable. Two of the double rooms on the first floor, each with its own bathroom, would be for Bed and Breakfast guests; downstairs, the front part, where books were now sold, had been the previous owner's antiques shop. Behind, the first-floor windows looked out at the high, green sweep of hills and woods.

It felt strange to live in a town where tourists came every day, a town that was famous. Matt was getting used to the mazy streets, the alleyways and shortcuts, the ramshackle castle sprawled over the hill in the middle with its flight of steps up, and the funny little shops tucked almost out of sight, selling things like pottery and dried flowers and hand-made jewellery. There was no WH Smith, no HMV, no PC World – none of the shops Matt took for granted. If you wanted those, Mum said, you wouldn't come to Hay.

As he cycled along Oxford Road, someone yelled, 'Oi, Lanky! Lanky Lanchester!'

It was Tig Jenkins, with Rob Howard as usual, at the entrance to the big car park. Matt looked over his shoulder, slowed, and pulled over. He hadn't liked *Lanky Lanchester* at first, but realised now that it was only a handy tag, the first thing they'd thought of. He wasn't particularly lanky, anyway: not like Fen, who was seventeen and very nearly as tall as Dad.

Back in November, when they'd come to Hay, Matt had been more anxious than he'd needed to be, about moving so far from his old school and friends. Tig and Robbo had been first to talk to him, so he'd teamed up with them; it made him feel safe from any teasing he might otherwise have attracted, as a newcomer. In some lessons he sat with a boy called James Kemp, or with Bryn Hughes, whose twin sister Sian was in another form group. The Hugheses lived out past Talgarth, on the farm where their father worked, and James even further away, so Matt didn't see much of them out of school.

'Want to hang out?' Tig said, wedging a foot against Matt's front wheel. He was wearing a black knitted cap pulled well down over messy hair; his face, as usual, was expressionless, compared with

Rob's, which was freckled, grinning, and somehow puppyish.

'What you doing?'

Tig shrugged. 'Nothing much.'

Matt looked at his watch. Only half-past seven.

'OK,' he said; though it got boring, hanging round the streets. In Milton Keynes there was a multiscreen cinema, there was the ski slope, there were shops open till late. Here there wasn't even a McDonald's, and the cafés closed early. Rob and Tig had been envious when he told them about the multiplex cinema at Milton Keynes, the snow dome and the skateboarding park. 'What made you come down here, then? Where it's front-page news if a cow sneezes?'

'What happened to you, then?' Tig said now, noticing the scuffed green marks down Matt's side and arm.

Matt felt silly. 'Came off my bike.'

'Yeah? You want to get one of those trainer bikes, for little kids,' Tig mocked. 'Till you can manage with two wheels.'

Leaving his bike propped against railings, Matt followed the other two into the car park. He thought of telling them about his crash, how the Land Rover had hurtled straight at him out of nowhere, how he'd thought he was a goner, then the baffling silence of being all alone in the empty lane – but by now it didn't seem convincing, even to himself. They'd call him screwy, or accuse him of making it up.

Rob handed him a stick of chewing-gum, and complained that his grandparents were coming to stay for Easter; Tig moaned about going to the dentist. Rob found a Coke can, empty and dented, and they kicked it around for a bit before Matt, giving in to the invisible, disapproving presence of Mum somewhere in his head, picked it up and lobbed it into the litter bin. Then Tig nudged Robbo and said, 'Hey.'

'What?' said Rob.

'Down there. White van.'

The car park was big enough for a hundred or more cars, but the small van seemed to hesitate, confronted by so much space. It moved on slowly, nudging into one of the marked bays near the meter. Then the door opened; an old man eased himself out, and unfastened the back doors to release a black-and-white collie.

'Who's that, then?' asked Matt.

'Don't you know Wil Jones?' Tig said, offhand.

'No, why would I?'

'Everyone knows Wil.' Tig made a sneery face. 'Shut it a minute.'

They sat on the wall by the steps to the craft shops, watching in silence as the old man whistled to his dog and clipped on its lead. At the meter he stopped to fumble in his pocket, taking some while to sort change.

'Senile,' said Tig. 'Well past it. You don't have to pay, evenings.'

Wil wore what Matt thought of as farmer clothes – corduroy trousers, sturdy boots, waist-coat, peaked cap with thick, iron-grey hair showing beneath. As he made his way back to his van, the dog bounded alongside, looking up at him eagerly. The man walked stiffly, as if his knees wouldn't bend.

I've seen him before, Matt thought. That walk. The bounding dog. It had been out on the hills, up towards Gospel Pass. Lots of people walked or rode bikes up there, on the open ground past the fenced-in fields, but he remembered this old man because he'd seen him more than once. He'd seemed to be searching for something, him and his dog, casting around among gorse bushes. Rabbits, most likely. The second time, as Matt had cycled down the narrow track, the man had stared, seeming to recognise him; then turned away with a muttered 'Afternoon'.

Now, after Wil had searched in several pockets before finding his car keys, and stuck the parking ticket inside the windscreen, he walked laboriously up the slope. Tig nudged Rob, and

Matt caught their quick interchange of looks. He knew they were up to something that didn't include him. Times like this, he still felt new, an outsider.

Tig and Rob ambled towards the entrance, Matt tagging behind. When the old man drew level, Tig suddenly called out, 'William.' Will-*yam,* he said it, in a harsh voice that made it sound like a threat.

Startled, Wil turned; he raised a hand to his cap. 'Evening,' he said gruffly, then walked on. Once people got old, Matt thought, it was hard to tell *how* old; but Wil looked older than Granddad had been, a lot older. Maybe seventy-something, maybe even older than that.

'Will-*yam,*' Tig called again, with the same growled emphasis. Rob giggled, and added some ape-like whoops.

The old man turned away. Whistling to his dog, he walked faster, reaching the pedestrian crossing. He made the dog sit at the kerbside before walking across, on into the alleyway opposite, and out of sight.

'Where's he off to, then?' Rob asked.

'Pub,' said Tig. 'My dad says he was in there last week, sat in the corner with a beer and a plate of chips. Must be missing his old missus.'

'What, she's died?' Matt asked.

'Nah. Hospital. 'Spect he's come from visiting.'

'She's gone gaga like him, I bet,' said Rob. 'Hope she never comes out.'

Matt felt uncomfortable. 'Why don't you like him?'

'*He* don't like *us*,' said Rob. 'Tried to set his dog on us, few nights ago. Gave us a right mouthful.'

'What for?'

'No reason,' said Tig. 'Just cos we were there.'

'Where?'

'Up where he lives. Up the Forest Road, long way up the hill. Show you, if you like,' Tig offered, in the couldn't-care-less way he had.

'It's all wrong he's walking around,' Rob said hotly. 'Ought to be in prison, and the key thrown away. He's a *murderer*.' He gave Matt a defiant look. 'Might not look like one, but he is.'

'You're winding me up!' Matt said. 'Who did he murder?'

'A boy. Boy our age. Years ago,' Rob told him. 'Stick together, lads. Safety in numbers, that's what my mum says.' But he couldn't look serious for long, and had gone pink under his freckles with the excitement of having news to tell.

'And he got away with it?'

'What d'you think? You can see for yourself –

he's walking round town, boozing in the pub.'
Tig gave a withering, down-his-nose look that
made Matt feel dim-witted. 'Anyway, that's it.
I'm starving – I'm going in. Hey, we'll go up
Dan-y-fforest if you want, tomorrow. Then I'll
tell you about it. Meet you here, half-ten? With
bikes.'

'Danny Forest?'

'Dan-y-ffo-rrest,' Tig said, exaggeratedly Welsh.
'Where he lives. Up over there.' He indicated the
hillside behind them, where Matt had been
exploring earlier.

'Might,' Matt mumbled, not sure. He hoped
Rob would stay – more might be got out of
Robbo, without Tig around – but Tig, pulling the
sleeves of his hoodie down over his hands as he
turned away, said over his shoulder, 'Coming?'
Like Tig's shadow, Rob followed him. They both
lived on the Hereford road: Tig's house was near
the supermarket, and Rob's a little farther out of
town.

The daylight was fading fast. The darkening
sky was streaked with cloud, a cool breeze was
sweeping down from the hills, and Matt felt
suddenly chilled. Two brushes with death, in one
evening! First, the roadside shrine with his
own initials; now the murder of a boy his own
age; and the killer, unaccountably strolling around

free, was a man he'd almost met, up on the hill! Things were beginning to feel – not dangerous, that would be a bit over the top, but, well, *unpredictable*. As if death, and ideas of death, were stalking him.

He wanted to be safely indoors.

THREE

Lanchesters

Matt was cycling, faster and more freely than he ever did in real life: gliding, almost flying. He was on a long stretch of lane with hedges either side, and something was pulling, pulling him, towards the dead tree that loomed large at the end of it, blocking the road. He'd have to turn either left or right to avoid whamming straight into the broad trunk, but he couldn't decide which, and the tree was tugging him like a magnet. At the last moment, choosing left, he wrenched at the handlebars with all his strength; then his heart jolted with fear as the Land Rover surged towards him. *Slam* – he felt no pain, but the bike melted away from him, and he came face to face with his initials, M.L., scored into the trunk, oozing something dark and sticky.

He tried to shout, but his throat was tight. Tried to look away, but the initials held his gaze.

18

Underneath M.L. he saw the numbers of a date, clumsily carved. He bent his head to look, but the figures blurred into nonsense.

What does it mean? What does it mean?

Find out, said a voice; a boy's voice, close by. He tried to turn, to see who had spoken, but his neck was rigid.

His bedside table swam into focus; he woke with his head rammed hard into his pillows and the duvet tangled around his legs. The room was already pale with morning light. *Find out.* The voice was so clear in his head that he could almost believe the boy was here in the room.

Blinking, he pushed himself up. Polly, the more sociable of the family's two cats, made a trilling sound and jumped up to the bed, butting her face against him, wanting attention. He stroked her, calmed by her warmth, and the deep throatiness of her purring.

Sometimes, still, he wondered where he was when he first woke up. Through his small dormer window he could see only sky. Normality settled around him, and he remembered that it was Saturday, and the first day of the holidays. As the dream faded, he wondered which parts were real and which he'd dreamed. He really had seen the initials on the cross, hadn't he? If he went back and looked, would they still be there?

As he got out of bed, he felt the soreness and bruising down his left side. He hadn't dreamed *that,* anyway. He dressed, and went downstairs.

The kitchen at Lanchesters was so big that everyone had to keep walking back and forth to fetch things: marmalade, cereals, hot toast from the toaster. Back in Milton Keynes, mornings had been frantic, with everyone snatching mouthfuls of toast or cereal in the small kitchen. Mum would be feeding the cats and organizing packed lunches, Fen fussing about homework, Dad looking for a phone number he'd jotted down somewhere, Matt making a last-minute attempt to get bag and books together. Now Mum and Dad's work was at home, and till the new term started Fen would be the only one going out every day, to her holiday job at the Granary café. Mum and Dad had taken to having breakfast together, sitting at the table, with a pot of proper coffee and sometimes even the newspaper. They were making the most of it, Mum said, before the Bed and Breakfast guests started coming, from Easter onwards. Dad's first job was to grout the tiles he'd put round the washbasins in the guest bathrooms.

'What's your plan for today, Matty?' Mum

always had a Plan pinned on the corkboard, a list of things she ticked off as she went through the day, and she expected everyone else to know what they were doing, too.

'Dunno.' Matt gulped cereal. 'Might go out on my bike, with Robbo and Tig.'

'That'll be nice,' Mum said. She took a sachet of Whiskas from the box; the cats, Polly and Perkins, jumped down from the dresser and began twining around her ankles, tripping her up as she reached for their bowls.

'Might be.'

'What's up with you?' Fen was neat in black trousers and red polo shirt, for work; her hair, which sprang wildly round her face when loose, was pulled back into a scrunchie. 'First day of the holidays – you don't sound full of the joys of spring?'

'Had a bad dream,' Matt mumbled.

'Oh, dear,' soothed Mum. 'What was it?'

'Can't remember.' Matt pretended to be intent on reading the back of the cereal packet. The dream – nightmare? – was still vivid in his mind, and he had the uneasy sense that it hadn't gone away, that it was waiting for him. Tonight, as soon as he let himself sink into sleep, he'd be back there: on the lane, hurtling towards the tree, the Land Rover, and the starkness of those black initials. If it was his future, if he'd been shown it for some reason, was it going to happen, no matter what? Or could he avoid it, simply by never going near the place?

'Help! I'm nearly late!' Fen clattered her bowl and mug into the sink. 'See you later.' She kissed Mum and Dad, gave Matt a friendly shove, and left.

Dad pulled on an old paint-covered sweater and went down to the cellar for his grouting stuff; the phone rang, and Mum answered it. From the extra-polite voice she was using, Matt guessed it was a Bed and Breakfast enquiry. She moved towards the big diary she used for bookings and reached for a pen, and at that moment Matt heard the brisk *tingaling* that meant someone had come through the shop door, from the street. 'Can you get that?' Mum mouthed at Matt, flicking through the diary pages.

Scraping up the last spoonful of cereal, he dumped his bowl in the sink with Fen's, then went through to the front.

An old man stood by the counter, looking at the books displayed in the glass-topped cabinet. Shocked, Matt registered corduroy trousers, padded waistcoat, iron-grey hair. *Wil!* No peaked cap today; no collie dog, either.

Wil looked at him. 'Morning, son. Is Mr

Lanchester about?' He looked even older, close up, and although he'd spoken only those few words, Matt heard the strong Welsh accent.

Matt stared, his throat dry and tight, just as in the dream. For a second he thought Wil must have come about last night: about Rob and Tig shouting at him in the car park. But what could he complain about? They'd only called his name. And why would he come to *Matt's* house, when Matt was the only one who hadn't shouted?

'What do you want?' It came out more rudely than he'd meant.

Wil cleared his throat. 'Got some books to sell. Out in the van.' He jerked his head in the direction of the street. 'Heard your dad was starting up, here, so I thought he might take a look. Doesn't matter if he's not around.'

'It's Mum does the books.'

'She here, then?'

Everything seemed to have gone into slo-mo; every question hanging in the dusty air, every word echoing. *We don't do business with murderers,* Matt thought of saying, but before he'd even wondered whether to speak the words out loud, Mum was behind him.

'Hello there! Lovely morning, isn't it? Can I help you, or would you just like to look round?' Cheerfulness radiated from her as from a sunlamp.

Wil looked relieved. 'Interested in buying, are you? I heard you're starting up.'

'Yes, that's right,' Mum said. 'I'll be pleased to have a look.'

'Boxes of stuff.' Wil looked doubtful again. 'Out in my van, there. I'll bring them in.'

'Lovely!' said Mum, like someone being offered a special treat. 'Matt will give you a hand. Matt, go and help Mr—?'

'Jones. Wil Jones.' Wil leaned forward and stretched out a strong, weathered hand, with ridged nails and a hairy wrist. Matt gazed in fascinated horror while Mum smiled, and shook hands – shook the murderer's hand! What might Wil have done with that hand? Matt imagined it gripping, squeezing, clawing, spattered with blood.

'Gillian Lanchester,' Mum said, smiling. 'And this is my son, Matt. Very pleased to meet you.'

Wil muttered something in reply, his eyes fixed on Mum's face. Matt wished Mum didn't look so *welcoming;* who could tell what thoughts might be going through Wil's mind? There was something about Mum that people immediately liked. Usually, that was fine with Matt, but this was different. He didn't want Wil to like her. Didn't want Wil here at all.

'Matt? Don't just stand there,' said Mum. 'Go

and help Mr Jones with his boxes – I'll clear a space.'

Reluctantly, Matt followed Wil out into the street. It had rained overnight; the air smelled fresh and damp. Wil opened the back doors of the van, which was parked awkwardly, with two wheels on the pavement and two in the road. Inside there were four cardboard boxes and, next to them, the black-and-white collie. Its amber eyes gazed at Matt; it thumped its tail.

'Stay, Jacko.' Wil hauled at the nearest box, and looked sidelong at Matt. 'Manage that, can you? You look like a strong lad.'

Matt didn't reply, lifting the heavy box; he was determined not to look directly at Wil, nor speak to him. In the back of van, besides the books, there was a plastic crate with tools in it, a roll of barbed wire, and some bits of orange twine. Stalks of hay and dried grass seeds were strewn about.

Mum propped the door open with a wedge, and cleared leaflets from the counter. By the time the fourth box was carried in, she was already going through the first.

She smiled at Wil. 'Looks like you're having a clear-out?'

He grunted, intent on examining something he'd found in his pocket; then he looked at Mum from under thick eyebrows. 'Got to make a bit of space, see. The wife's been in hospital for a while. Hip operation. She'll be home soon. She won't manage the stairs for a bit, so she'll be needing the downstairs room to sleep in.'

'Oh, I see,' said Mum. 'You must be looking forward to having her back.'

Wil shuffled his feet on the worn carpet. 'Books and books and books we've got. This is only the first lot. Most of them not touched from one year to the next.'

'Well, you've got some interesting stuff here, Mr Jones,' said Mum. Matt had seen her sort books before, brought in by customers. Most of them, the ones she didn't want, went back into their box or crate; the ones she *did* want were stacked on a pile on the counter. This time, she was stacking nearly all of them, and the box was almost empty. He glanced at the pile she was making, four books wide. They didn't look specially interesting to him, but then very few old books did. He glanced at his watch: nearly time to meet Rob and Tig, if he was going. But he couldn't leave Mum alone with a murderer, especially as he'd had no chance to warn her.

'All these wonderful children's books!' she was saying. 'Your children must have been very lucky, Mr Jones, to have such a library at home.'

Children? It hadn't occurred to Matt that Wil might have had children of his own. Wil the boy-killer ought to have been an evil hermit living on his own in the woods.

Wil shuffled his feet, saying nothing.

'And you've kept them all!' Mum went on. 'That's brilliant. You must be sorry to part with them, but lots of people are on the lookout for titles like these. I'll certainly make you an offer. A few of them, though, might be quite valuable.' Mum put her hand on a separate heap she'd made, of six or seven. 'I'm no expert, but I don't want to do you out of whatever they're worth. You might do better to try one of the specialist children's booksellers. Or would you like me to get them valued for you?'

'I haven't time to go traipsing all round town.' Wil sounded impatient. 'I'll leave them with you – maybe bring more boxes down, if you don't mind.'

'No, please do!' Mum told him. 'I'll do some searching on the Internet. As for these others – let's see – I could offer you, say, sixty pounds for what's here?'

Wil pursed his mouth. 'Call it sixty-five and I'll say yes.'

'Well—' Mum tilted her head to one side. 'Sixty-two, then.'

'Sixty-three.'

'Sixty-two fifty, that's the best I can do.'

Wil nodded. They shook hands, both looking pleased with the deal. Matt knew that this was how buying and selling went on in Hay; it looked more fun, haggling, than simply handing over a marked price. But Wil would have settled for less, he thought; Mum needed to sharpen up. He was thinking of trying it on, to raise his pocket money: 'Stick on an extra couple of quid and you've got yourself a bargain.' If she thought some of those books were valuable, why hadn't she bought them off him for a fiver, *then* found out how what they were really worth?

Mum took notes and coins from the till and placed them in the none-too-clean palm of Wil's hand; Wil nodded thanks, and pocketed the money. Matt fingered the dust jacket of *The Swiss Family Robinson*, impatient for Wil to be gone. Opening the cover, he read inside *To Owen, Happy Christmas, with lots of love from Mum and Dad,* in sloping handwriting, so old that the ink had turned brown.

'I'll be back later today, or tomorrow. Good day to you.' The door-bell *tingaling*ed as Wil shut it behind him.

Mum gave a sigh of happiness as she contemplated her purchases. 'That was good!'

Mum was never going to make money at this, Matt thought. She liked buying books better than selling them. But he didn't say so; there was something more important on his mind.

'I'll get these priced and shelved straight away,' Mum said. 'What a nice man. Didn't you say you were going out?'

'Mu-um, you think *every*one's nice!'

'What's wrong with that?' She was turning on the computer. 'I'd rather see the best in people, unless there's good reason not to.'

'What if there *is* good reason?'

'Well, do you know one?'

'That old man was in town last night,' Matt told her, 'going to the pub. Tig and Robbo know him. They told me he killed a boy, and got away with it.'

Mum glanced up. 'I don't believe it!'

'Why would anyone make up something like that? Mum, you shouldn't let him come in the shop! He's a *murderer* – you never know what he might do.'

Mum laughed. 'That'd be really good for business, wouldn't it – banning local people from the shop?'

'You've got to admit it's odd, though,' Matt persisted. 'Like you said – there are dozens of bookshops in Hay, and two that sell nothing but kids' books. Why wouldn't he try those first? Why come here?'

'Maybe he *has* tried there first – it's up to him,' Mum said. 'Anyway, I don't believe it. If that man's a murderer, I'm a duck-billed platypus.'

FOUR

Dan-y-fforest

'What kept you?'

They were waiting, bored, down by the car park wall. Tig looked at Matt with his odd, expressionless gaze; Rob grinned.

Matt skidded to a halt. 'Customer in our shop! And you'll never guess who it was?'

'Mickey Mouse?' Rob guessed. 'Spider-Man?'

'Come on, then.' Tig opened a pack of chewinggum. 'Amaze us.'

'It was Wil,' Matt told them.

'Hey, hot news!' Tig turned to Rob, with the funny smile he had that reached only one side of his mouth. 'Man visits bookshop in Hay. Hold the front page.'

'No, but *Wil*,' Matt insisted. 'Selling off kids' books. His old lady's coming home from hospital soon, he said, and he's having a clear-out.'

'So the old boy's on his own up there for a bit longer?' Tig said.

'S'pose so. Anyway—' Matt couldn't help thinking that they hadn't seen the *point* of this '—there was my mum, in the shop, doing business with a murderer!'

'Ooh, dodgy. Blood on her hands. Stolen goods, I bet!' Tig gave a spoofy shiver. 'Come on, then. If he's here in town, he'll be doing his shopping – good time to give his place the once-over. We going, or hanging round here all day?'

He and Rob mounted their bikes. Matt followed them out of the car park and out to the Brecon road, soon turning left onto Forest Road and the sign that said *Capel-y-ffin, Unsuitable for Coaches*. This was the route that climbed through twisty lanes to the open moorland of Gospel Pass, the way Matt had cycled on his own. Once, in winter, Dad had driven the family all the way up and over the pass, stopping for a walk on the blustery heights where sheep and ponies grazed.

'What about that boy he killed?' Matt called, while they were still on a level stretch of lane and cycling with little effort. 'You said you'd tell me about it.'

'Yeah. Better than that, we'll show you the actual place.'

What? Matt's imagination raced, picturing a hidden grave, or scattered bones, or a rope dangling from a tree. Their tyres were zizzing along damp tarmac; Matt felt a buzzing in his ears as he realised, with a sense of inevitability, what they were going to show him. He'd approached from a different direction last night, down the hill; they were coming from the left bar of the T. But there it was.

The dead tree. The cross. M.L. The daffodils, beaded with rain.

So it wasn't for him. It was someone else; another boy, a boy who'd died a long time ago. He felt something lightening in his head, a sense of freedom. Still, those initials . . .

They came to a halt, positioning their bikes in a reverent semicircle.

'This is where? I saw it yesterday. Gave me a bit of a shock,' Matt told the other two. 'M.L. Matt Lanchester. Like seeing my own grave.'

Tig nodded. 'Yeah, right. But M.L. stands for Martin Lloyd, as well.'

'Martin Lloyd? The boy Wil murdered?'

Rob scraped a foot on the ground; Tig said, 'It wasn't so much an actual *murder*. We wound you up a bit about that.'

'What, then?'

'Drunk driving,' Tig said. 'Hit and run. Manslaughter, I s'pose you'd call it. Wil had been to the pub, like he usually was, and on his way home he goes smack into boyo on his bike.'

33

I know, Matt thought. If he closed his eyes he would live it again, see the vehicle heading straight for him, hear the engine. Fear clutched at his throat; he gripped the handlebars more tightly and concentrated on bringing himself back to the present, his feet standing firmly on tarmac, the sun's faint warmth on his back. Everything was normal. But he had a strong feeling that if he turned his head to look behind him, there'd be another boy standing there. A boy of about his age, thin, with straight dark hair that fell over his forehead, and dark brown eyes.

'Wil?' His voice came out hoarsely. 'That was Wil?'

'Who else are we talking about?' Tig gave him a disparaging look. 'Course it was Wil. He never told anyone. Kid wasn't found till next morning, with well bad head wounds. Died in the ambulance on the way to hospital.'

'So Wil could have—' Matt tried to take this in. 'You mean, he drove off? Just like that? Left the boy lying here in the road? Why didn't he—'

'Call the police?' Tig supplied. 'Well, why d'you think? There'd have been whisky on his breath – they wouldn't even need a Breathalyzer. He legged it fast as he could.'

'But that's—'

'Yeah.'

'Nearly as good as murder,' Rob said, with relish.

'I don't get it.' Matt frowned at his handlebars. 'If Wil did that, and everyone knows, how'd he get away with it? Why isn't he in prison? And how come *you* know all about it? You can't tell me you remember, if this happened ages ago?'

'Not all that long. Eight or nine years. My brother was in Martin's class at school – *he* remembers. Everyone knows,' Tig said lightly. 'It's just they don't talk about it.'

'But didn't the police—'

'No witnesses, see,' Tig said, 'out in the lanes, like this. I bet Wil went home and cleaned up any evidence that was on his van—'

'Blood, bits of brains,' Rob said helpfully.

'—and bashed his bumper straight, if it was dented. Then all he had to say was he'd been up in the fields with his sheep all night. Why'd the police have him down as a suspect? Could have been anyone. Fact is,' Tig said, 'he got away with it. He's laughing. Let's get on up there – if he's in town he might still be chatting up your mum.'

'What're we going to do?' Matt felt uneasy.

'Just have a look. Like I said, we'll show you where he lives. *Dan-y-fforest,*' Tig said, with the exaggerated Welsh singsong that sounded like mockery. 'Up in the forest where nobody goes.'

Up in the forest where nobody goes. It sounded like

35

a line from a song; repeating and repeating itself in Matt's head, a tune forming around the words as he cycled uphill behind the other two. The landscape was wilder here, hill-pasture grazed by sheep, with the misty heights of the Black Mountains rearing beyond. Well away from town, there was only the occasional farm, cottage or tumbledown outbuilding to be seen. When Matt thought they'd got past the end of all human habitation, and it would only be sheep and crows from now on, Tig turned abruptly down a dirt track to the left. This track forked: Matt saw large farm buildings on the right; to the left, a grey roof among trees. A signpost, with paint worn and peeling, pointed to Ardwyn Farm one way, Dan-y-fforest the other. Tig took the left turn, which led to a rickety gate; behind it, Matt saw a cottage, slate-roofed, with a porch sagging beneath the weight of ivy. Beside the gate there was a stile with the yellow arrow that meant Public Footpath. It pointed to the left of the house, past an open-sided barn, which contained sacks of stuff and rusty old clutter: an ancient wheelbarrow, a heap of chains, pitchforks, shovels and rakes. A few chickens, chestnut-coloured or black, pecked about the yard.

'Here we are. Wil's place.' Tig left his bike lying on the grass. He nodded towards the stile. 'See, we can go in if we want. He can't stop us.'

Rob and Matt dismounted too. The gate was lopsided on its hinges; the bushes and shrubs in the garden looked in need of cutting back. As Tig approached the stile, a sudden loud barking startled all of them. Wil's black-and-white collie, Jacko, hurtled down the path and stopped abruptly, facing the gate. Tig stepped back in alarm. *He's frightened of dogs,* Matt registered. *He likes to think he's hard, but he's not sure about dogs.*

'He's OK, aren't you, Jacko?' Matt, used to Grandad's two Labradors, wasn't nervous; dogs usually seemed to like him. The collie came to him and jumped up with front paws resting against the gate, and Matt reached out a hand to rub his ears. Mum sometimes said that he'd get himself bitten, doing that with dogs he didn't know, but Matt thought he could tell whether or not a dog was friendly. Jacko was, looking up at him with amber eyes.

'If the dog's here, so's Wil,' he told Tig in an undertone, though he couldn't quite see how – no white van had passed them on the lane. At the same instant he saw it, parked behind bushes on the far side of the barn. Wil must have come straight back from the bookshop, instead of staying in town for shopping, as Tig had supposed.

And now here was Wil himself. Leaning on a stick, he came out of the front door, onto the porch, and peered around. 'Yes? What is it?'

Matt, too slow, found himself the only one still there by the time Wil's gaze focused; the other two had dodged out of sight behind brambles. Something pinged into the ivy, quite close to Wil; a stone, it must have been, thrown by Robbo or Tig.

Wil stepped out to the path; then his eyes swivelled to Matt, and fixed on him. Matt was pinioned by indecision, aware of Robbo's muffled laughter close by. He thought of dodging out of sight, but felt himself held, pinned by Wil's gaze. Then Wil came forward, one step more, and seemed caught in confusion.

'Is it? It's you, isn't it?' he said, his voice husky. 'It really is you. After all this time.'

'I—' Matt began. There must be some mistake. He still had one hand buried in Jacko's cool fur. Jacko turned his head from him to Wil and back again with a little *whuff* of contentment. With that footpath sign on the stile, people must walk through here all the time; Jacko must be used to strangers. But Wil thought otherwise.

'He knows you!' he said, with a wavery smile. 'He knew you before I did! My eyes aren't what they were. Don't stand there, boy – come on in! Gwynnie,' he called over his shoulder, apparently to someone indoors. 'Gwynnie, come and see!'

Another stone whizzed past Matt's ear and into

38

the ivy. Matt couldn't help looking round at where Robbo was hidden.

'What's that?' Wil stared; Jacko barked, bounding over to investigate; there was a scuffle in the bushes. Matt caught a flash of Robbo's ginger hair as he and Tig tried to slip away beside the hedge. Wil, suddenly decisive, said something to the dog, a single word Matt didn't catch. At once Jacko, alert, was over the gate and down the track, skulking low. 'Hey, get off!' Tig shouted, in alarm; but Jacko was clearly a professional working dog, not an attacker. Within moments he had rounded up the two boys like sheep and brought them back, keeping close behind them, watching their every movement. So anxious was Tig for the dog not to nip his heels that he was almost trotting.

Now Wil was angry; he strode to the gate, brandishing his stick. 'You two again!' he shouted. 'I told you not to come back here! Now clear off, or I'll—'

'Yeah?' Tig jeered. 'Or you'll do what?'

'I'll call the police,' Wil returned. 'You've got no business up here.'

Tig laughed. 'Yeah, get 'em round, why don't you?'

'It's a free country!' Rob taunted. 'We've got more rights than *some* people ought to have!'

Matt slipped away, heading for his bike. He didn't like this.

Another vehicle was coming: a four-by-four Discovery, moving slowly along the track, while chickens squawked out of its way. 'Run for it, Robbo,' Tig muttered. All three boys hauled at their bikes, clambered astride and pedalled off, passing the Discovery, which stopped at Wil's gate. Glancing back, Matt saw that the side window was open, the driver leaning out to hear what Wil had to say.

Rob whooped with laughter as they pedalled hard back to the main lane, his voice lifting away on the wind from the hills. At the next gateway, Tig veered off the road and came to a halt, the others close behind.

'That was good!' Rob panted. 'Daft old git!'

It was mean, Matt thought. *We shouldn't have done it.*

'Mental,' said Tig. 'Gone senile.'

'We could do him for assault, if you ask me,' Rob went on. 'Setting his dog on us – coming at us with that stick!'

'You should have seen yourselves,' Matt told them. 'Toddling along, gormless as sheep in a pen! If Wil's entering Jacko for a sheepdog trial, he could use you two instead of sheep.'

Rob grinned, and swigged at his water bottle. Tig's face tightened.

'Tell you what, though,' he said, leaning on his handlebars. 'That stuff about *it's you, it's really you*'—he put on a weak, whiney voice that was nothing like Wil's—'*after all this time . . .* what's he on about?'

'Screwy,' said Rob. 'Head case. Doesn't know what day of the week it is.'

'You know what, Lank?' Tig looked directly at Matt. 'I reckon you ought to do it.'

'Do what?'

'Go in. Next time he asks. Go in, and see what happens next.'

Matt looked down at his foot on the pedal. 'Why?'

'Well,' Tig reasoned, 'you'd be doing him a favour, wouldn't you? Not doing anything *bad*. You could tell, the way he said it – he really, like really wanted you to go in. It'd make his day.'

'But he thought I was someone else,' Matt said. 'And I'm *not* someone else, so how would that cheer him up?'

'Obvious,' said Robbo. 'He thinks you're Martin. Come back to haunt him!'

Matt's thoughts flicked back to the moment by the tree, the strong presence of the boy behind him, watching. Martin? It could only be Martin. He gripped his handlebars and stared at the ground, pushing Martin's face out of his mind.

'That's rubbish,' he mocked. 'Why'd Wil want to invite me in, if that's what he thinks?'

Rob gave him a pitying look. 'Come on, Lank. So's he can say sorry? Cos he wants to think Martin's alive and walking about, 'stead of lying in the road with his brains splattered out?'

'Stop going on about brains!' Matt said, impatient. He'd seen the drawings Robbo liked doing in his rough book at school – gory pictures of gunshot victims or axe-murderers, spattered with gobbets of red.

Tig gave his humourless laugh. '*Talking* about brains isn't going to *give* you any more of them, Robbo.'

Matt looked sharply at Tig. Rob went to a Special Needs teacher twice a week, instead of going to lessons with the rest of the form. Robbo grinned, not seeming to mind. But Tig was like that: he knew how to get at people. Knew their weak spots.

And now I know one of his, Matt thought, thinking of Tig's alarmed expression when Jacko bounded up. *That might be useful.*

'What I don't get,' Rob went on, unabashed, 'is how he got back from town – I mean, he didn't pass us on the way. You sure it *was* him in your shop, Matt?'

'Course I'm sure!'

'Obvious,' Tig said. 'He comes round the Llanigon way, even though it's longer – cos he doesn't want to pass the place where IT happened. Think he wants to see that, every time he goes out in his van? Late attack of guilty conscience, if you ask me.'

Matt prised a thorny bramble stem from his sleeve. That much made sense, at least.

'Anyway,' Tig pursued, making his front wheel nudge Matt's. 'What about it, Lank? How 'bout we go back, say tomorrow? Round lunchtime?'

'Dunno,' Matt hedged, pushing off into the lane.

Tig was heading down the way they'd come, back past the T-junction, the tree, the M.L. cross. Matt didn't want to go there again. When they reached the place, he made himself look straight ahead at Tig's navy hoodie and windblown hair, in case the boy should be there by the roadside, waiting to catch his eye. *You were a witness*, Martin would tell him silently. *You saw. You know. What are you going to do about it?*

FIVE

Granary

'Matty, come here now and tidy your room!' Mum called from the top floor. 'I asked you to do it yesterday!'

She was trying to do what she called a quick whizz round with the Hoover, while Dad looked after the shop; but the Hoover had stopped on the attic landing, between Fen's room and Matt's.

'I can't even see the *floor*,' Mum complained, as Matt climbed the narrow stairs. 'Honestly, you're chalk and cheese, you and Fen!' She held Fen's door open to show him inside. Everything was meticulously tidy, the bed made, with red and purple cushions neatly arranged at the pillow end; her desk held a reading lamp, a ring-binder and a stack of textbooks, and an office-tidy in which he saw a box of staples, paper clips compartmentalized according to colour, gel pens, Pilots and highlighters, and pencils ready sharpened. On her wall she had a chart of the Periodic Table, a map of Antarctica and a printed speech from *Macbeth*, illustrated with a floating dagger. Swot, or what? She must be the only teenager in the world who got up early every day of the holidays and did an hour's schoolwork before breakfast and her work at the café, and she'd most likely be at it again this evening, after they'd eaten. Matt's homework would stay firmly in his school bag till the last day before term started. Why spoil a good holiday?

Pitched against such opposition, he'd never do better than poor second in the tidy-bedroom stakes. Mum fetched him a couple of bin bags and he made a start, half-heartedly sorting through the clutter of magazines, socks, topless felt-tips and empty CD cases that littered his floor.

He felt restless. Something was pulling him away from home, out into the lanes and hills; up, in his mind, towards Dan-y-fforest, to the lonely cottage. He wasn't sure about Tig and Robbo, whether he wanted to get drawn in to their taunting. Maybe Wil did have a guilty secret, maybe he'd done something terrible and unforgivable – but three against one, three boys against a muddled old man, was too much like bullying. Then he remembered Wil's quick command to Jacko, and the dog's instant control of the situation, and thought: *Well, three against two, then. So if I don't join in with them, it'll only be two against two. That evens it out a bit.*

'See you half-one, same place, if you're up for it,' Tig had said, when they'd parted yesterday. He gave the impression that Matt's choice was to turn up or bottle out. *Let them think that,* Matt told himself, reaching under his bed for a stray football sock; *I couldn't care less.* But another part of him argued that he *did* care. Not so much now, but when they were back at school. Being Tig's mate, everyone seeing that Tig thought he was OK, had helped him to feel part of things. Tig didn't have to do much to impress, just *be.* He was the sort of boy who could sum up a new supply teacher in an instant, and could silence the class prat with two words muttered under his breath. All Matt had to do was get into Tig's slipstream and be carried along, skimming the currents of school life. Really, he liked Bryn Hughes more than either Tig or Rob. Bryn was cheerful, and easy to be with, and wouldn't lead him into situations he'd rather not be in – like the stone-throwing up at Wil's. Matt felt uncomfortable, remembering that; he knew all too well what Mum would say, if she found out. Bryn had suggested that Matt might go over to the farm one day, but it hadn't happened yet. The other snag with Bryn – apart from living so far away – was that, out of lessons, he spent a lot of time with Sian, his twin. Matt didn't want to go round with a *girl*.

Grouting sounds and the endless yak-yakking of Radio 4 had been coming from the larger of the two guest bedrooms all morning. By the time Matt was lugging his dirty washing downstairs, Dad emerged, pleased with himself.

'There, that's done! Thought we'd go round to the Granary for lunch, the three of us. You around this afternoon? Fancy earning some extra pocket money? I could do with a hand clearing out the cellar, and loading stuff for the tip.'

In the busy café, Matt glanced at his watch. Ten past one. That settled it, then: he wasn't going with Tig and Robbo today, and now he had the excuse of helping Dad all afternoon.

The café, smelling of bread and spicy sausage and coffee, was self-service. Leaving their coats at a table, they joined a line of people with trays, and looked up at the chalked boards. Mum waved at Fen, who could be glimpsed in the kitchen, through a hatch. She looked lightly steamed and a bit pressured, giving them a quick smile as she wielded an enormous teapot. Being Fen, she'd marshalled the waiting cups and mugs into ranks, their handles precisely aligned.

'Have whatever you like,' Mum told Matt.

Matt chose jacket potato with beans and cheese. While Dad dithered, Matt's attention was diverted to someone ahead of him in the queue. For a second he thought it was Mr Donaldson, who taught PE at the Milton Keynes comprehensive. Then the young man laughed and turned his head, and didn't look much like Mr Donaldson after all, apart from being tall and athletic, with light brown hair. He was buying lunch with an older woman – his mum? – who was taking a long time choosing between various kinds of herbal tea. Fen came out to the till and added it all up. When the woman found that she hadn't enough in her purse, her son took a twenty-pound note out of his wallet and handed it to Fen. 'Oh, thank you, Adam,' said the woman, pronouncing it in the Welsh way, Ad-am; 'I'll pay you back later.' Fen counted out Adam's change, looking up at him with keen-eyed interest. Noticing that, Matt thought he might tease her about it later.

Mum paid, and they carried their trays through to the side room where they'd bagged their table: just as well, as there were few places left.

'Tourists, mostly,' said Mum, looking around. 'Browsers. Book buyers. Good for business. I must bring some of my leaflets in here, when we've got the website online.'

'We need to plan some days out,' Dad was saying, as they unloaded their plates and cutlery. 'It's a shame to live in a place like this, and not get out and about. Once I've got the house sorted, we'll clear off for the day now and then – over to the Brecon Beacons, or a castle, or canoeing on the river. There's all sorts of things we can do.'

'Yeah, yeah.' Matt dug into the fluffy inside of his jacket potato. He'd heard it all before. '*When* you've done all the painting, and got the electrician in, and the plumber, and done the garden and the cellar and the kitchen.'

'It does feel a bit like painting the Severn Bridge,' Mum said, 'taking on such a big house, and such an old one.'

'You mean the Forth Bridge,' Dad pointed out.

'Why? Doesn't the Severn Bridge need painting?' Matt asked.

'It's a saying,' said Dad. 'By the time you reach the end, it's time to start again at the beginning. I haven't even *looked* at the guttering yet.'

'But we're not making ourselves slaves to it,' Mum said firmly. 'It'll all get done, in time.'

While his parents talked, Matt noticed that Adam and his mother had taken the small table in the corner. Bits of their conversation drifted across; Matt tuned his ears, blocking out Mum and Dad. Adam seemed to be describing some kind of mountain expedition, camping out in snow. He looked the outdoor type, fit and tanned, and was younger than Mr Donaldson – nineteen or twenty, perhaps. As he talked, he moved the salt and pepper pots and sachets of ketchup to make a kind of diagram; his mother nodded, following. 'See, the tents are *here*, in this dip, and this is all boulder field, and then there's a huge drop.' He demonstrated, slicing a hand past the edge of the table. It must feel good to be so grown-up and independent, Matt thought. You could do what you wanted, go wherever you liked.

When they'd all finished eating, Dad cleared plates on to a tray. 'Anyway, Matty, we'll definitely have some time out over the holidays. Fen too, if she can get a day off.'

'I don't know about you, but I'm thinking about sticky toffee pudding,' Mum said. 'Want some? We've got time.'

Twenty minutes later they were walking back up Lion Street. 'Am I seriously expecting myself to *work*, after all that food?' Dad said ruefully; then, as they reached the bend by the antiques shop, 'Hey – looks like we've got a customer.'

Matt's heart thudded. Wil's white van was parked half on and half off the pavement, exactly where it had been yesterday. And if Wil was here, and Robbo and Tig had gone up to Dan-y-fforest and found the cottage unattended, what would they find to do there? He didn't like to think too closely about that – but, more urgently, he didn't want Wil to see him!

'Come on, Dad.' He led the way round the side of the house. 'Let's start on the cellar, before you go off the idea.'

SIX

Where Nobody Goes

'*No!*' Matt yelled.

It was the most tremendous effort to get out any sound at all; something was clogging his throat, almost choking him. He spluttered, flung out his arms, and was suddenly awake, staring into darkness. Slowly, the lighter shape of the window came into view, and his curtains, stirring gently in the draught.

The dream-picture was still vivid. It had thrust itself to the front of his mind, shocking him awake: a body, *his* body, lying spread-eagled on a road, next to a crumpled bike. And the head – he'd heard somewhere that you couldn't see colours in dreams, not really, but he could have sworn that the head was horribly split open, bright blood spilling – and worse than blood, like one of Robbo's gruesome drawings. 'Help me!' he – the body – had been trying to shout, but the Land Rover, with Jacko looking out of the back window, had driven off fast, the sound of its engine echoing in his ears.

Now silence: so loud that it was almost frightening. He clicked on his bedside lamp, and his room – computer, jeans slung over a chair, trainers on the rug, laces trailing – sprang into view, bright and ordinary.

The phrase came into his head again: *Up in the forest where nobody goes* . . . It repeated itself, fitting into a tune, over and over, till Matt couldn't get it out of his head. There wasn't a forest up at Wil's, in spite of the name; only belts of trees between fields, and bordering the lanes. But . . . *where nobody goes* . . . If you killed someone, you crossed a line: you couldn't undo the terrible thing you'd done: you were on your own, in a place of no return. What Will had done was cruel, cowardly, *wrong. But what,* Matt thought, *am I supposed to do? What's it got to do with me, anyway? I'm going to forget all about it.* He turned over, thumped his pillow into shape, and was about to turn off his light again. Then stopped, his hand stretched out for the switch, on realising that the boy was there again, as if he'd stepped from the back of his mind into full view. He wouldn't be ignored. Matt closed his eyes and there he was: Martin, it had to be, thin, dark-haired and serious, looking intently at Matt, willing him to do something.

'What?' Matt asked. He opened his eyes, realising he'd said it aloud. What was wrong with him? Talking to a dream, to a dead person! What had got into him?

He was wide awake now. Sitting up, he looked around his unnaturally tidy bedroom; his cube clock showed half-past two. Might as well read for a bit: he propped up his pillows and settled. For once, though, Anthony Horowitz failed to grip, and he found himself reading the same page twice. Needing to pee, he went down to the bathroom on the first floor. From Mum and Dad's room he could hear, faintly, Dad's snoring.

Going back up, he noticed a crack of light showing under Fen's door. She wasn't working *now*, surely? Even Fen had to sleep!

'Fen?' he called softly. No answer. He rapped lightly on her door; still nothing. Turning the handle, he pushed the door ajar, just enough to see in.

Fen was at her desk. The lamp illuminated her face as she looked intently at the papers in front of her, giving no sign of having seen him. She wore a strappy little top in purple edged with mauve, and matching trousers of satiny stuff – it looked to Matt like something a girl might wear to a party, though he knew it was her birthday-present pyjamas.

'Fen? What you doing?' he whispered.

'I haven't even started yet,' she murmured, in a strange, slurred voice. 'Deadline—' followed by something he couldn't quite make out; then, again, 'Haven't even started yet.'

'Haven't started *what*? Fen, what're you on about?'

For a moment he wondered if she was drunk – Fen, who rarely went out in the evenings, whose idea of a social life was to go round to her friend Anna's for a bit of History revision! – before it occurred to him that she was actually asleep, though her eyes were open.

'Fen?' he said, more sharply. This time she blinked, turned slowly to look at him, and gazed in surprise; she rubbed her eyes, and pushed her hair back from her face. 'Oh—' She gave an embarrassed little laugh, then, shivering a little, reached for her dressing-gown and shrugged it on.

'What're you *doing*?' he repeated.

'Nothing! It's just – I do this sometimes. Wake up in the middle of the night and think it's time to get up.'

'But it's half-past *two*!'

'Is it?' Fen said vaguely. She picked up her hair-brush and frowned at herself in the mirror. Matt tweaked her duvet out of its heap, and sat on the end of her bed.

'What do you do, then – sit there writing course-work essays in your sleep?'

'I wish! No – usually I wake up after a bit, and find myself sitting there, and go back to bed. Afterwards I'm OK. Sometimes I creep down to the kitchen and make hot chocolate. You haven't heard me, have you? I'm pretty good at not waking everyone up. It's just'—she gestured towards her desk—'there's so much to do!'

'That's stupid! You can't do anything about it in the middle of the night!' Matt said. 'Besides, it's the *holi*days.'

Fen gave a wry smile. 'Wait till you're in Year Twelve, and everything counts for AS-Levels.'

'Hmm.' Matt couldn't see himself getting *that* worked up about it, even then.

'Look,' Fen said urgently, 'you won't say anything to Mum and Dad, will you? I don't want them fussing.'

Matt nodded. 'Did you say hot chocolate? If you're going to make some—'

'OK. Wait here.' Fen put on slippers; on her way out of the door, she added, 'What are *you* doing awake, anyway?'

'Oh, nothing,' Matt said.

He heard the merest creak of stair treads as she soft-footed downstairs. As he waited, the dream surged back into his mind. He couldn't shake off the feeling that Martin was inside his head, trying to speak to him. As soon as he closed his eyes, the face was there, pale and serious – looking for him, wanting his attention.

Martin Lloyd.

Martin was quiet, the sort of boy who spent a lot of time on his own. He liked drawing, quick scribbly sketches, or more detailed pictures he worked on when there was no one around.

How do I know that? Matt thought.

There was no answer; and no more dreams of Martin that night. Full of hot chocolate, Matt slept dreamlessly, or at least without remembering what he had dreamed.

In the morning he made a decision. The only way to find out more was to go up to Wil's again. But not with Robbo and Tig, with their jeering and stone-throwing. This time he was going alone.

SEVEN

Fox

'Mum,' Matt asked at breakfast, as casually as he could, 'what did Wil want yesterday?'

'Wil?'

'I mean Mr Jones,' he amended. 'You know, who brought the books.'

'*Oh*, you mean the axe murderer!' Mum gave him a look. 'Now, what was it? Ah yes, I remember. He was after books on arsenic poisoning.'

'What's funny?' Matt huffed. 'You think I'm making this up? He really *did* kill someone. He knocked down a boy in his car, a boy about the same age as me, and the boy died.'

Mum's face changed. 'Oh, how awful. Poor man.'

'Poor *man*?' Matt was outraged. 'What about poor *boy*?'

'Imagine having to live with something like that.'

'Imagine having to *die*!'

'Who's died?' Fen came into the kitchen, dressed for work.

'No one. Fen, love, you look tired.' Mum got up from the table to put more bread in the toaster. 'I hope you're not overdoing it?'

Fen caught Matt's eye: *Remember. Don't say anything.* 'I'm fine,' she answered.

In the hall the phone rang; Mum, hurrying to pick up, was beaten to it by Dad, who was on his way out of the front door. 'Matt, it's for you,' he called. 'Bryn.'

'You doing anything today?' Bryn said, straight to the point. 'We're canoeing on the river this afternoon – you can come if you like.'

'Great, what time?'

'We'll come and pick you up. Our brother's at home – he's taking us. Two o'clock?'

'Great. Thanks.' Matt put the phone down, and told Mum, who was pleased. Now he had the morning free; Dad had gone to the supermarket, and would then look after the shop, while Mum went to choose books from a house clearance in Hereford. Matt was on his own.

He knew what he was going to do. He went out to his bike and cycled out of town in the Brecon direction, then left up Forest Road. At Martin's shrine-tree he stopped, pulled over to the verge and looked up at the initials he shared with Martin.

'Well, I'm on my way,' he said aloud. 'Is that what you want?'

Immediately he felt silly, talking to a tree. There was no answer, not even a silent one, and Martin's face obstinately refused to come into his thoughts. It was for Martin he was going, though he was losing the sense of resolve that had brought him this far. If Wil's van was gone, if Wil were down in town again, he could simply have a look round, peer in through the windows, maybe, then leave. Reconnaissance, he could call it. *Time spent in reconnaissance is seldom wasted:* that was one of Dad's sayings.

He cycled on uphill. The sun, breaking through hazy clouds, was almost warm on his face; the day felt full of spring. If he didn't stop at Wil's, he could go on towards Gospel Pass, and be all alone up there. He looked ahead, to the gorse-clad, brackeny slopes that rose to a shoulder of ground, dotted with sheep. That would be better, the open hillside, away from bad feelings and guilt.

But when he reached the turning, what he'd said to Martin – not exactly a promise, but still he'd said it – made him take the forked track and look over Wil's gate. The white van, as before, was parked by the outbuilding; a thin plume of smoke rose from the cottage chimney. Barking startled him: with Jacko around, he was never going to lurk unseen.

Jacko bounded over, pleased to see him; a few moments later Wil followed across the orchard grass, ducking beneath low branches.

What now? Matt's throat was dry while he rubbed Jacko behind the ears. What could he say? What reason could he have for coming back?

But Wil didn't look at all surprised; only sad and resigned. 'It's been a bad night, boy. My fault. No one's fault but mine.'

'What happened?'

Wil opened the gate, gesturing towards the orchard. 'Lost one of the hens, her favourite. How she got out the ark, I don't know. Only moved it yes'day, thought they was all safe shut in, see! Must have left one out. Jacko started barking, about nine, only I was too slow to let him out. By the time I heard the commotion, it was too late, all died down. I had a quick look round with my torch and went back to bed. Found her just now, over by the hedge.'

He stopped at the corner of the cottage, by a compost heap. It was a simple wire enclosure half full of weeds and vegetable scraps; on top was a black, bedraggled bundle of feathers, its neck twisted. Matt saw strong scaly legs, a closed eyelid like a lizard's, and the yellow bill still open from its last gasp.

'What happened?'

61

'Fox got her. Varmint!' Wil clenched his fists. 'I'll shoot it if I see it again! Now how am I going to tell her? Her favourite, that is, that little black one. And they haven't been laying well, last week or so – they know, see. Know she's not here. I'm sorry, Gwynnie, truly I am.'

'Gwynnie?' Matt echoed. Wil had called the name last time, and he'd been surprised to realize that Wil wasn't alone here after all. Maybe Gwynnie was his daughter?

Now Wil looked at him with watery eyes. 'No, Gwynnie's not here, boy. Didn't I tell you? Not till Sat'dy. Comes home from hospital then. Come you in and I'll make us some tea.'

'Well, I—'

So Gwynnie was his wife? For the first time it occurred to Matt that the old man might really be mad: talking to someone who wasn't here.

And he's got a gun – he said he'll shoot the fox—

Matt didn't have to stay. He could go back to his bike and spend the morning helping Dad, then go canoeing this afternoon. He needn't give a reason; he could just leave. Now.

But he didn't. He followed Wil round to the back door, with Jacko padding along behind.

He was doing everything wrong. PSE lessons at school were always telling you about *stranger danger*: never go off with an adult you don't know, always tell someone where you are. No one knew where Matt was; no one except Wil, and here he was, entering a house with a man who was not only a stranger but behaving very oddly, and who had a gun, and had already killed a boy and got away with it.

On the doormat, Wil levered off his boots, toe to heel, and left them outside; Matt copied, prising off his wet trainers. He followed Wil into a low-ceilinged room, cool and dim, dominated by a large stone hearth, with the embers of a fire smouldering in the grate. It was old-fashioned and cluttered, smelling of wood-smoke and tobacco-smoke and bacon. The floor was stone tiled, with raggy rugs over it; there were two unmatched armchairs and an uncomfortable-looking wooden-backed settee facing the fire, and a dresser, displaying flowered plates. Light filtered through thin curtains; a jug of faded, papery daffodils stood on the high sill. Jacko, with a little sigh, flumped down on the hearthrug, nose on paws.

'Sit you down,' said Wil, waving Matt towards the nearest chair. 'I'll make us some tea.' He stumped off into the small kitchen adjoining.

Matt didn't want tea. What he wanted most was to be back outside, on his own, free. He sat awkwardly, moving two cushions aside. It felt like going back a hundred years; he'd never been in a place like this. He heard the gush of a kettle filling with water, and the clatter of crockery, and Wil breathing hard as he moved around the kitchen. A clock measured the moments with a heavy, reluctant tocking. Carpeted stairs, a narrow flight of them, led up between this room and the next; that, Matt supposed, must be the room Wil was clearing of books, as there were none in here. He looked more closely at the dresser. It held rows of plates, all patterned with leaves and flowers; also, a china dog ornament, a box of Milk Tray, and some orange pellets, cylinder-shaped. He recognised those: on a walk with Dad, he'd seen them scattered at the edge of a wood where people had been shooting pigeons. Gun cartridges!

He looked around for the gun – a rifle, it'd be – but his gaze fell instead on a framed black-and-white photograph on the top shelf.

A boy. A boy of about his age, half-smiling; hair flopped over his forehead. His dark eyes looked straight at the camera, straight at Matt. *Martin?* Could it be? Dressed in school uniform – V-necked knitted jumper and striped tie – he was neat and self-conscious, posing. It looked like one of those official photographs schools did at the start of each year.

Was it Martin, or wasn't it? Matt looked again, uncertain now. Whenever he tried to catch the face in his mind, the face that was always watching him, it blurred out of focus. *This* boy, in the photograph, was flesh and blood, alive. His gaze held Matt's, so that it felt like meeting someone he knew.

It didn't make sense – Wil keeping a photo of Martin, the last person you'd think he'd want to remember. It seemed like a kind of trophy, the way old-fashioned hunters used to mount stags' heads on their walls. Wil's victim. What was going on?

Get out. Get out, while I still can.

But Matt stayed in the chair, gripping its frayed armrests as his eyes searched the room. There must be more photos, more clues. But the biggest clue had to be Wil himself, who at last shuffled back into the room with a tray, which he lowered carefully to a side-table. There were two mugs of tea, a bowl of sugar, and squashed-fly biscuits on a plate.

'Your favourites, see.' Wil lowered himself stiffly into the other chair. 'I always ask Gwynnie to get some, in case.'

Why did he think that? Boasters were Matt's favourite.

Five minutes, long enough to drink the tea, then I'm going.

He tried a cautious sip, then put the mug back on the tray. He didn't even *like* tea much, and this was twice as strong as he'd ever had it, and much too hot to drink.

Wil took a big slurp of his. 'I always said you'd come back. Gwynnie says I'm only disappointing myself, but I knew. He'll be back, I keep telling her, I know he'll come back one day. And see, I'm right! Wait till she sees you!'

Matt shuffled in his seat. Wil must really be as crazy as Tig and Robbo said. At first, outside, Matt thought Wil had recognised him – after all, it was only two days since they'd met in the shop – but no. It was like last time; Wil had him muddled up with someone else.

'Why did you—' Matt began; the words dried in his throat. 'Why didn't you stop?'

'What's that?'

He had to say it again, getting more and more self-conscious, his face glowing hot to the tips of his ears. 'Why didn't you stop?'

'Stop?' Wil's face creased in puzzlement.

'On the lane. By the tree. Where the cross is.' He could see that Wil still didn't understand. 'Where Martin – where Martin died. Martin Lloyd.'

'Martin? Martin Lloyd?' Wil repeated. He stared at Matt intently; his face darkened. 'But you can't know – that was after, a long time after—'

'I do know. People know. He's dead, and you're not, and it's all wrong!'

66

'Wrong? You're telling me what's wrong and what isn't, young scoundrel?' Clumsily, Wil got to his feet. 'Is that – is that why? Is that why you've come back?'

Matt couldn't meet his eye. He got up, glancing towards the door. Why had he started this?

'Answer me! I said, is that why you've come back? You're ashamed of me, is that it?' Wil's voice rose; Jacko was instantly alert, awaiting an instruction. 'That's what you've come to tell me? If that's it, you'd better go. Go on!'

Matt hesitated; Wil reached out for the stick that rested against the table.

'Did you hear me?' His voice was a hoarse whisper. 'I said go!'

'OK, OK.' Matt's eyes were on Jacko. 'I'm going!'

He blundered out into the orchard. He wasn't at all sure what he'd stirred up here, but he didn't like it. Wil pursued him as far as the gate, and Jacko stayed close to Matt's heels, to make sure he really did leave. In the lane, Matt scrabbled to pick up his bike, feeling hot and awkward. He gave one glance back. Wil was standing by the gatepost, almost collapsed against it.

'No!' he called to Matt. 'I didn't mean it – please, come back!'

No way! Matt pushed off, heading downhill. From the bushes ahead, he heard: 'Come back!

Please, come back!' like a ghostly echo of Wil's cry. The hairs rose on the back of his neck; then he saw the two bikes in the gateway, and a flash of red.

Tig and Robbo.

Although he'd wanted to avoid them yesterday, he was pleased to see them now. He steered off the lane, braking.

Tig punched his arm. 'Good on yer, Lank! Nice one, infiltrating the enemy!'

'What happened?' Robbo was perched on a stile. 'Did you wind him up?'

'I don't know,' Matt said, conscious that *he invited me in for a cup of tea* wasn't going to sound too impressive. 'The creepy thing is, he's got a photo of Martin on his sideboard-thing.'

'What?' Tig looked at him keenly. 'Has he? How d'you know it's Martin?'

Good point, Matt thought.

'I just know,' he said lamely.

'How sick is that?' Rob gloated. 'Keeping a photo of his victim? Like he's proud of it? See, he *is* raving mad. Evil.'

'So what'd you do, when you got inside?' Tig pursued.

'I asked him,' Matt said brazenly, 'I asked him why he drove off and left Martin lying there.'

Rob giggled. 'And what'd he say?'

'Went ballistic! Grabbed his stick and told me to

clear off out of it – then next minute he's all *Come back! Come back!'* Uncomfortably, Matt felt that he was betraying Wil, but then, why should he care? Telling the other boys made it seem less disturbing, more laughable. Wil had killed Martin; nothing was going to change that. He hadn't even tried to deny it.

'Screwy,' Robbo said, making a loony face: eyes wide and staring, mouth grimacing lopsided, tongue lolling out. 'Should be in a mental home if you ask me.'

'He's got a gun in there!' Matt went on. 'I saw the cartridges. He says he's going to shoot a fox that got one of his chickens.'

'Aw, shame,' said Tig; Robbo looked at him sidelong, a grin spreading.

Matt felt hot. 'Was it *you*?'

'Us?' Tig said, all innocence. 'We might have let some of his hens out, but how was we to know Mr Big Bad Fox'd come strolling along? Animal liberation, that's what it was. We thought nice little Henny ought to have a nice little stroll round the nice big field.'

'We only took eggs,' Robbo added. 'Not hens.'

'But that's stealing!'

'Ooh dear, is it?' Tig mocked. 'Shock horror! Better give 'em back, Robbo, you thieving little git.'

'Bit late now,' Robbo said, grinning. 'If you want

them, they're down there in the ditch, only a bit scrambled.'

'I've had enough.' Matt began to push back into the lane. 'I'm going home.'

'Not so fast.' Tig reached out and grabbed his handlebars. 'You weren't thinking of telling anyone about this, were you?'

'No. . . ' Matt stalled.

'You sure? Not Mummy and Daddy?'

Matt shook his head; Tig looked at him for a moment, considering, then said slowly, 'We'd better make sure about that. Wouldn't want something to slip out by mistake. I've got an idea.'

EIGHT

River

Arriving home, Matt let himself in at the front door. 'Hello?' he called, getting no answer; then, hearing the murmur of conversation in the shop, he went through the kitchen and round, to tell Mum he was home.

'Is that what Matt said? A boy about his age?'

It was Dad's voice. Matt stopped in the doorway.

'Yes – after he told me the man was a murderer! Obviously it's not true.' Mum sounded as if she had her head in a cupboard; he had to strain to hear. His ears felt hot and tingly.

'What if it is?' Dad went on.

'I don't think so,' said Mum. 'It's one of those things kids get hold of, and blow out of all proportion.'

'Well, I don't know. These things happen.' Dad was moving closer; Matt stepped back quickly. 'What if there's a grain of truth in it? And another thing – should we stop Matt going so far on his bike, the way he does? Those winding lanes, miles from anywhere – all those sharp bends and blind corners. What if *he* got hit by some mad driver?'

Matt held his breath. He liked going out on his own; it gave him a sense of freedom that he found nowhere else.

'We can't wrap him in cotton wool!' said Mum. 'He's pretty sensible. And he's got these friends now, Tig and Rob. He's usually with them. *And* this other boy, Bryn, the one he's going canoeing with.'

Pretty sensible! If only she knew!

'Well, that's something,' said Dad. 'He sometimes seems like a bit of a loner. There's nothing wrong with that, but – it's good he's made friends. D'you want these crates taken down to the cellar?'

Matt heard the bump of boxes being stacked. Furtively, he slipped back into the kitchen, then opened the door noisily and called, 'Hello!'

'Hi, Matt!' Mum appeared from the shop, brushing dust from her jeans, pushing a sleeve back to look at her watch. 'Is that the time? I'd better do something about lunch. You're going out at two, aren't you?'

Following Bryn to the black Fiesta parked outside, Matt was surprised when the driver, turning round to smile hello, was someone he recognised: the young man he'd seen in the café.

'You don't know Adam, do you?' Bryn said. 'Our brother. He's taking us.'

Matt climbed into the backseat, next to Sian. 'Saw you yesterday, in that Granary place,' he told Adam. 'My sister works there.'

Adam nodded. 'Oh, yes? The shy one, would that be?'

Fen wasn't really shy, but Matt had seen how she'd been almost dazzled by Adam. Matt felt rather in awe of him, too, remembering how he'd talked about some mountain expedition. Adam filled the car with his presence, his light hair brushing the roof, his long arms and legs barely fitting into the driver's space. The twins weren't much like him in appearance: small, but very active and quick. They weren't identical, but both had the same pale-straw-coloured hair and thin pointy faces.

Adam, Bryn told Matt, was training to be an outdoor pursuits instructor at a place called Plas-y-Brenin in North Wales, and was home for Easter. He'd already done the Duke of Edinburgh Gold Award and was, according to Bryn, always planning mountain walks, river trips and caving expeditions. 'Great for us,' Bryn added, 'cos he's always looking for victims – I mean people to take with him.'

The canoeing centre was next to a road bridge a few miles upriver from Hay. Bryn and Sian had done it before, so – once everyone had been fitted with life jackets and helmets – they were given a canoe together, while Matt shared with Adam. The canoe felt alarmingly light and wobbly as he stepped gingerly in. He was anxious not to make an idiot of himself, but soon learned how to handle the paddle, how to slide it into the water and pull deep rather than splashing ineffectively at the surface. After a while they swapped places, so that Matt sat at the back and tried steering, avoiding the low overhang of branches at one side and the shallow pebbly reaches on the other. Adam said he was doing well, and the twins shouted encouragement. There was something mesmerizing about the flow of the river, swollen by recent rain, the soft rippling sound it made, and the weedy, watery smell.

It almost – but only almost – drove away the worries that crowded into his head. He tried to swat them away, like flies out of a kitchen; they'd have to wait till later. For now, he was enjoying himself, and it felt good to be with people who only wanted to have fun together.

They beached the canoes at a point downriver where Adam's friend David picked them up with a trailer. Afterwards, Adam drove them all back to

Ty-Mawr Farm for tea. The Hugheses lived in the cottage that went with their father's job, and the twins showed Matt around – the sheep with new lambs, their working dog Ifor, who was very like Jacko but getting old and due to retire, and the farmer's daughter's pony, which Sian was sometimes allowed to ride.

'Can Matt come with us when we go up Pen-y-Fan?' Bryn asked Adam, when it was time for Matt to go home. 'We are going, aren't we? D'you like hill-climbing, Matt?'

Matt nodded. 'Penny Van? Where's that?'

'In the Brecon Beacons, not far,' Adam told him. 'It's a long walk, steep in places – a mountain, we're talking about. We won't rush, but it's quite a climb. Will you be OK with that? Have you got a good pair of boots? Waterproofs? Fine, then. I'm not sure which day yet – Sunday, I was thinking, if the weather holds. The twins can phone you.'

Matt remembered to thank everyone, and the twins' father drove him home. Mum was in the kitchen, making a casserole for dinner, but had got sidetracked into reading while it simmered.

'How was it? Did you have a good time? I've been sorting through Mr Jones's books. Some interesting stuff he's brought.' She lifted a saucepan lid to prod the potatoes. 'Hurry up!' she told them. 'I'll be late.'

Matt grunted, unlacing his trainers. He couldn't seem to get away from Wil. 'Late for what?'

'The drama group.'

'Drama group? But you've never—'

'No, I've never! That's why I want to do it now!' Mum said, with a lift of her chin. 'I've always liked the idea, and now we're here it seems a good way of meeting people. No point moving to a place like this if I bury myself in work all the time. Don't worry – I won't embarrass you. I'll only do small parts – can't see myself as leading lady. Or I might help backstage. Another ten minutes, I think,' she added to the potatoes, turning up the gas. 'Did you have tea at the twins'?'

'Yeah, cake and stuff. But I'm hungry again now.' The casserole smelled good, meaty and tomatoey and spicy.

Mum nodded. 'Anyway, I was telling you about Mr Jones's books – quite a collection, he's got – a shame to part with it, I told him. Welsh language, some of it, so I've no idea if that's valuable or not – and a lot more children's books. A first edition of *The Owl Service,* with its dust jacket – that must be worth a bit. Don't suppose you've heard of it, but it's a real classic.'

'What about that?' Matt gestured towards the folder she'd been reading from.

'Oh, yes. That's a bit of an oddity.'

'It's not what you'd call a book,' Matt said, picking it up. It was a beige folder, with a wad of thin pages inside, hole-punched and held in place by knotted green string.

'No, I know. It looks like someone's manuscript – a story someone's written, and typed up.'

The Story of Tommy Jones, said the label on the front, typed by what looked like an old-fashioned typewriter, the print uneven.

'Doesn't say who wrote it,' Matt said, leafing through the pages.

'No, I know. That's why I wonder if *Wil* did. I don't suppose he meant to bring it – it's not the sort of thing I could sell. When he comes again, I'll see if he wants it back. Don't think I'll read it after all – it might be private.'

Matt turned to the first page, curious. He couldn't imagine Wil sitting down to write a story, and this was quite a long one.

'Tommy? Tommy Jones?' he queried.

'Mmm. I thought Tommy might be Wil's son – but none of the books have Tommy's name in them. A few are *To Owen,* but never a Tommy. Owen had a lot of books, that's for sure,' Mum said. She tasted the casserole, then reached for the pepper-grinder and twisted it vigorously over the brew.

'Who are you talking about?' Dad, coming in, went to the sink to wash his hands.

'Mr Jones. The man who brought the books.' Mum gave him a look; Matt saw the quick, meaningful glance that passed between them, and knew it referred to the conversation they'd had earlier. 'You know, I feel sorry for him,' Mum went on. 'It must be hard for him – all on his own, and visiting his wife in hospital every day. I expect he'll have to look after her when she comes out, do all the shopping and so on.'

'You don't feel sorry for me when *I* do the shopping!' Dad said, turning round to look for a towel.

'No I don't! It's all hands on deck here – but a bit different for men of his generation. Anyway, Matty!' Mum lifted the saucepan lid to poke the potatoes again, releasing a waft of steam. 'You haven't told us about the canoeing yet.'

Hours later, Matt was wide awake in bed. The title of that story was in his mind, clear and confusing. *The Story of Tommy Jones* . . .

Who was Tommy Jones, and why had Wil written a story about him?

He turned one way and then the other, yanked the duvet up to his ears, immediately felt too hot and threw it back, unable to make sense of the puzzle that was tying his brain in knots.

And a bigger worry: why had he agreed to do

what Tig told him? Why had he got himself into this? If Tig and Robbo wanted to hang around Wil's place causing trouble, why not leave them to it? They weren't real friends, he knew that. It was all a game to Robbo, and Tig only wanted to use him.

'You'll be doing the old boy a favour, really,' Tig had reasoned. 'He wants to see Martin, doesn't he? – well, you can *be* Martin. I'll tell you what to say. Tomorrow, two o'clock, car park?'

'It'll be like those role-play things we do at school!' Rob had said, wriggling with anticipation.

'That's right,' said Tig. 'Therapy.'

But whatever Tig had in mind, it wasn't therapy, Matt knew. He wanted to stir up memories. He wanted Wil to be punished.

'What am I doing?' Matt said aloud, into the darkness of his bedroom.

Silence. Silence, and a faint creaking from the room across the landing.

He knew what to expect, this time. He climbed carefully out of bed, crept to Fen's door and knocked softly. He didn't expect her to answer, but immediately she did. 'Matt?'

He went in. She was sitting, as he expected, at her desk, but fully awake and in her dressing-gown: pen in hand, an A4 pad with the top page half-covered in her neat writing, textbooks open in front of her.

'What you doing?'

'What's it look like?' She glared at him. 'Writing a history essay.'

'*Now?*'

'What's wrong with now? No one's going to disturb me, are they? – at least, I thought they wouldn't.'

'Fen, you are *sad*.' Matt shook his head. 'When do you sleep? Why can't you go out to clubs and parties like other girls do?'

'I don't know any clubs and parties. Anyway, this is more important.' She looked at him anxiously. 'You won't tell Mum and Dad, will you? You promised!'

'Well—' He hesitated. It was all very well promising, but what if Fen ended up making herself ill, or having a nervous breakdown or something? People did, when they drove themselves the way she did. It was an *obsession*, all this work. She'd never, he knew, get to the point where she could say: 'Right, that's it! All finished,' and pack away her books and folders. There would always be more to learn, to revise, to do again, do better. He'd read once about a Greek myth where someone had to keep pushing a heavy stone to the top of a hill, only to watch it roll down to the bottom and heave it up all over again – that was Fen. She was a perfectionist, Mum said; she thought she'd failed if she got anything less than grade A for her schoolwork. She'd spend hours and hours on an essay, put it in a smart plastic folder ready to hand in, then convince herself it was rubbish and start all over again.

'OK, OK. I'll get the hot chocolate.' Fen pushed back her chair.

'That wasn't what I—'

'What, then?'

'What I mean is, wouldn't it be *better* if they knew?'

'How would that help?' She put on what Mum called her muleish expression; they all knew how stubborn Fen could be when she made up her mind. 'They'd only start interfering and trying to take me to the doctor, like I'm a psychiatric case or something. It's only a bit of homework, for God's sake. You'd better not tell them, Matt – I mean it. You promised.' She faced him over the back of the chair. 'OK? Now you.'

'What d'you mean?'

'You're going to get yourself in trouble if you hang around with Luke Jenkins's brother. You must know that?'

'*Luke* Jenkins?'

'You know who I mean. Tig, or whatever you call him.'

'Tig's all right.' Matt fiddled with the sleeve of

his pyjamas. 'And I don't know Luke.'

'But you do go round with Tig. Anna saw you going off with him and that other boy, on your bikes. What d'you get up to?'

'Nothing much. Riding around.' Matt felt sure he was going red.

'Where Tig goes, there's trouble. Anna knows. He's just like his brother. I don't know Luke and I don't want to, but Anna does. So do most people in my year. He left school two years ago, but he's got a bad reputation. And his little brother sounds nearly as bad.'

'But that's not—'

'There was something about a boy in her road, back in primary school,' Fen went on. 'Tig got him so scared, he was having nightmares and pretending to be ill, so he could stay at home. His parents had to go in and see the Head. I've seen him around at school, too – seen the way he intimidates smaller kids. Why d'you hang around with *him*? Haven't you got other friends – what about that Bryn, the one you went canoeing with?'

'I can have more than one friend if I want.' Matt's voice came out with a stubbornness to match Fen's.

'Well yeah, but – OK, then.' Fen crossed her legs, with the air of someone who has made up her mind.

'OK what?'

'You don't tell Mum and Dad about me working late – I don't tell them what I know about Tig Jenkins. Deal?'

'All right. Deal,' Matt mumbled.

'Hot chocolate?'

He nodded, and she set off down the stairs; he heard her slow and careful progress, avoiding the second step down, the one that creaked.

'I don't mind if you stay here for a bit, if you want to read or something,' Fen told him, returning with two steaming mugs. 'Long as you're quiet.'

'OK.' He fetched his Alex Rider book, but again found his thoughts wandering. Owen, Tommy, Martin. Three identical faces – he had no way of knowing which was which – seemed to circle round his brain, frowning at him, wanting him to *do* something, solve something – it was doing his head in! He'd have to read that story. Wil had written it, and it was *The Story of Tommy Jones* – there might be something in it that would make sense.

Mum had said it might be private, but she'd looked at it all the same – there couldn't be any harm in borrowing the folder till morning, to see if he could find any clues.

'Just fetching something,' he told Fen, and crept

83

down the two flights of stairs, through the kitchen, where Polly and Perkins yawned at him from their basket, disturbed for a second time. He switched on the lights, and went through to the shop. The light from the kitchen was enough to show him, behind the counter, three boxes of books on the floor, and the beige folder on top of one.

He couldn't read it in Fen's room, in case she saw and asked questions. 'I'm going to sleep now, OK?' he told her, collected his drink, and went back to bed.

The Story of Tommy Jones, he read.

This is the story of little Tommy Jones, aged five.

NINE

The Story of Tommy Jones

This is the story of little Tommy Jones, aged five.

Tommy Jones was a lively, happy little boy who lived in a town in the Rhondda valley. His father was a miner, but his grandparents were farmers, in a faraway valley in the Brecon Beacons.

At the end of summer, at the Bank Holiday weekend, Tommy and his father set out to visit the grandparents. They had a long journey, by train, and then four miles to walk from the station. Tommy was already tired by the time they reached the valley.

Coming to the mountains was an adventure. Tommy loved books, and stories, he had heard of faraway places, of desert islands and palm trees, of icebergs and glaciers, and of tropical jungles where monkeys hooted and hummingbirds hummed. In his picture books he saw children very different from him, he saw little black boys, and mischief-eyed Chinese girls, Indian children in turbans, and Eskimos in furs. He wondered how the world could be such a huge and bewildering place, and could contain so many different people.

This outing to the Brecon Beacons seemed quite far enough for him. While they walked, Tommy's father told him tales of this place, where he had grown up. Already they could see the clear line of the mountain ridge, and the summits high above. Tommy's father told him how, as a boy, he used to roam on the hillsides, where he loved to hear the singing of larks, the mewing of buzzards and the croaking of ravens. He loved the springy heather and the soft bog-grass and the paths that climbed ever more steeply through bracken and rocks and boulders to the high summit of Pen-y-Fan. Once, with his father, who was of course Tommy's grandfather, he had walked all the way up, climbing and climbing till his legs ached and his lungs were parched of breath. Reaching the top at last, he gasped with astonishment as he saw how the land was scooped away, falling and falling down sheer cliffs that made him dizzy to look at them, as if a giant had taken an enormous spoon, the most enormous spoon imaginable, and sliced away a huge mouthful of mountain.

Next to Pen-y-Fan, beyond a dip in the summit ridge, high and misty above Tommy and his father as they walked, was the peak called Corn Dhu, which means in English, Black Horn. Tommy's father told him this, and Tommy imagined the same fierce giant, having eaten his fill of rocks and stones, blowing his horn to signal a warning to all the other giants and ogres who lived in the mountains round about. The horn notes would sound loud to his ears but would be quickly snatched away by the wind.

'The wind gusted and buffeted and blew up there,' Tommy's father told him, 'and I held tight to your grandfather's hand for fear of being blown right away. I could imagine myself turned into a kite, soaring and diving over the valley, whirled and twirled by the wind.'

It was a warm, sunny afternoon, and everyone was looking forward to the Bank Holiday. No one could have foretold how dreadfully the day would end.

Not far from Tommy's grandfather's house, there was a place called the Login, where soldiers camped for training on the hills, and on the nearby rifle range. There was a canteen there at the Login, and as Tommy was already hot and tired from the walk from the station, his father bought him lemonade and a pennyworth of biscuits.

While they were eating and drinking and resting in the shade, Tommy's grandfather came up the path, with Tommy's cousin, William John, a lad of thirteen.

'You run back home and tell your grandmother they're nearly here,' said Grandfather to William John. 'She'll get the kettle on ready.'

'I'll come too!' shouted Tommy, suddenly full of

energy again. And he ran off up the narrow valley behind his bigger cousin.

'Take care!' shouted Grandfather.

Tommy soon began to tire again, for the way was steep and rocky, and there were places where the stream had to be crossed on a rickety plank with no handrail. He began to feel frightened. For a while he struggled to keep up with William John, but then he grew unhappy and began to cry.

'I'm going back to my daddy!' he wailed.

'You go, then,' said William John, knowing that he would be quicker without his small cousin toiling behind. 'I'll be back as quick as I can.'

But little Tommy Jones never rejoined his father and grandfather. When William John bounded back along the path, having completed his errand, he was astonished to find that the little boy was nowhere to be seen. Of course they all started calling and searching without delay, but there was no answer, though they all yelled and yelled until they were hoarse.

If it seems impossible that someone could get themselves thoroughly lost on a sunny day in August, you must remember how confusing things can be in the mountains, and how very suddenly the weather can change. What starts out as a balmy day in summer can soon feel as chill as November, or as raw as February, when the wind changes or the mists come down. Many a walker, even a strong and experienced walker, has come to grief through underestimating this difference, and the speed with which conditions can change.

Tommy Jones was trying to make his way back to his father and grandfather, but when he reached a junction in the stream he was puzzled, and turned along a rocky little path. Here he made his mistake. Instead of turning towards the farm, he was heading up another branch of the narrow valley, one that wound upwards to the open hillside, and passed no buildings at all.

Tommy did not at first notice the mist spreading over the hills, like a giant's slow breath. He did not at first notice that the path rising before him was no longer clear, but lost in pearly haze. He did not at first notice that there were no landmarks in sight, no farmhouse, barn or cowshed, or that everything was swimming in the same pale gloom.

Then he heard a voice calling him. 'Tom-mee! Tom-mee!'

The voice came from higher up the hillside.

'Who is it?' he called. It must be William John, come to find him.

'Tom-mee! Tom-mee!'

'I'm here!' he called, and he turned away from the path, and struck off into the rough grass.

'Tom-mee! Tom-mee!'

He walked and he called, he called and he walked, but no matter how far he followed, the voice seemed just as far away. And now there was another voice, harsher and cackly, that warned, 'Go back! Go back!' then broke into chuckling, as if all this were a good joke.

Tommy only gave a whimper in reply. He was almost too frightened to move. He stood still and looked around him, and realised that he was quite lost. The ground was rough and tussocky, and he could see no path at all.

'Go back! Go back!' called the second voice, although that voice too was ahead of him, higher yet up the slope.

Now that he had stopped walking, Tommy began to feel cold, shivering in the smart sailor suit he was wearing for the visit. His boots were new, and thin-soled, and his feet were aching. It may have been August, but it was already dusk, and mist clouded the fading light and moistened the air with fine rain.

What should he do? If only he had stayed with his father, he would be safe and warm now, in Grandfather's house, and would soon be getting ready for bed. How lovely that would be, to lie warm and snug in his attic bed, while the grown-ups chatted below!

'Don't leave me!' he wailed to the two voices. 'Help me find the way!'

And he looked around in a panic, first one way and then the other, and could see no difference, no landmark to guide him. He was lost, all alone, small and tired and shivering on this vast hillside, with no one to hold his hand and lead him safely to Grandfather's. He began to cry, and was frightened all the more by the sound of his wails.

'I'm here,' said another voice, close by. 'I'll help you.' He felt a soft, warm touch against his leg. It was a dog, a tall, grey, rough-coated dog. Tommy's father had told him about a dog just like this, who had lived on the farm when he was a boy. That dog was called Gwilym. But Gwilym had died long ago, and was buried in the orchard. Tommy's father had never said anything about Gwilym being able to speak, so Tommy began to wonder if he were dreaming. If so, maybe it would turn out to be a nice dream after all.

Gwilym looked at him with calm, amber eyes. 'Come with me,' he said, in his gruff, wooffy voice. 'You're lost! You've come far out of your way, little boy, far too high up the hill, where you should never, never come on your own. But I'll lead you down.'

Tommy laughed, and buried his hands in Gwilym's rough fur, for warmth. He was safe now. No one knew their way around the hills better than Gwilym. Father had told him that.

'Follow me,' said Gwilym. 'Don't worry. I'll never let you out of my sight.'

And the big dog led the way downhill through clumps of sedge-grass. Tommy followed, stumbling sometimes, but Gwilym was careful not to get ahead in the mist, stopping every few paces to look over his shoulder and make sure that Tommy was with him. Soon they were on a narrow path between boulders, and heading down the slope. The voices, now behind them, still called out 'Tom-mee! Tom-mee!' and 'Go back! Go back!'

'Who's that, calling my name?' Tommy asked.

'That's not your name. It's only the buzzard mewing,' said Gwilym. 'Take no notice.'

'And who's that telling me to go back?' Tommy asked.

'That's only the red grouse calling,' said Gwilym. 'Take no notice.'

'But you're real, aren't you?' Tommy asked.

This time, Gwilym did not answer. His shape ahead, in the swirling, hazy mist, was dim as a shadow. Tommy had to look very hard to see him at all. Suddenly he felt weak with tiredness, and hungry, and faint. A nearby dip in the ground looked so tempting that he called to Gwilym, 'Wait!' He sank down on the grass.

Gwilym gave a low growl. 'No!' he gruffed. 'That is the one thing you mustn't do. You're tired, but you must keep walking. Lean on me, I'll support you, and my fur will warm you.'

'Please!' Tommy pleaded. 'My legs are so tired! I'll walk better if I rest a minute.'

'No!' Gwilym barked. He nudged at Tommy's legs with his muzzle and tried to push him up.

'Please!' Tommy begged again, and this time he did not wait for an answer, but rolled over and curled himself for sleep. The springy turf was like the most comfortable mattress he had ever known. Gwilym gave a little whine, then settled too, and curled close to Tommy's body, to warm him. Tommy gave a sigh of contentment, and buried his hands deep in the dog's warm fur. Even the rain was only a fine mist in his face, gentle and soothing.

Gwilym could easily have slept too, but did not allow his eyes to close. He lay staring alertly into the gloom, to the path down to safety. He heard Tommy's soft breathing and knew that the boy was asleep. Just one minute – two minutes – Tommy looked so peaceful, lying there with a little smile on his face, that Gwilym did not want to disturb him. But he knew that he must. He got to his feet, and nuzzled at Tommy's arm.

There was no response. Gwilym nuzzled again, then pawed at Tommy's jacket, then licked his face.

Tommy's face was cold. There was no breath, no warmth, no life. And Gwilym knew that Tommy would never breathe again.

He raised his muzzle and gave a long, mournful

howl that echoed to the top of the mountain.

'Tom-mee! Tom-mee!' called the buzzard, not caring.

'Go back! Go back!' called the red grouse, not knowing.

Gwilym had promised to stay with the boy, never to let him out of his sight, and he kept his promise. He lay there in the hollow, next to poor, dead Tommy, and sometimes he wept, and sometimes he howled, and sometimes he padded round in circles before settling again. For he had failed in the task he had set himself. He had failed once and failed for ever.

A long, long time later, when many days had passed, he heard voices. He looked, and saw a procession coming towards him, ponies, and people. Tommy's parents, and all the people from neighbouring farms, had been searching the lanes and bogs and ditches for Tommy, and had almost given up hope of finding him. Where had he gone? Had he wandered far away? Had he drowned? Had he been kidnapped, and taken right out of Wales? By day and by night they searched; the mists and the rains cleared, and the skies turned back to the clear blue of summer.

'Tommy! Tommy Jones!' the searchers shouted, but only the lonely cry of the buzzard, as it wheeled in the August sky, answered them.

And at long last they found him: high on the slopes

above the farm, beneath the giant's spoon-scoop of Pen-y-Fan, huddled in a hollow in the ground, heather for his pillow, as peaceful as if asleep in his own little bed.

What they did not see, what none of them could see, was the ghost-grey shape of Gwilym, loyally keeping company, for he had never left Tommy in all the days he had lain there.

Poor Tommy was carried away and buried, and the mourners mourned, and the weepers wept, and the wailers wailed.

All this happened a long, long time ago, but the spot where Tommy Jones took his last sleep is marked to this day, so that travellers can pause and remember his sad story. If you go there, and think of him, you will pause and look around you and be astonished at how high up the mountain that lost little boy's last journey brought him. If you listen carefully, you may hear the call of the buzzard, and the croak of the red grouse. But what no one sees is the ghost-grey shape of Gwilym, the faithful; and what no one hears is the sorrowful howl he makes when the moon is bright and clouds scud above the hills.

TEN

Whitewash

By the time Matt woke up, sunlight was filtering through his closed curtains, and the sounds of voices and cars outside told him that Tuesday was well under way.

'Come on, sleepyhead! Wrong time of year for hibernating.'

Matt hadn't even realised that Dad had come into his room, he'd been so heavily asleep. Dad yanked the curtains open to let the sun in, while Matt rubbed his eyes blearily and squinted at his clock. Twenty to ten!

'Fen's already gone to work – we've had breakfast, an hour and a half ago. Feel like giving me a hand whitewashing? It won't take long.'

The *Tommy Jones* folder was on the bedside rug. Matt quickly shoved it out of sight, under the bed, before Dad asked what it was. It broke his dream; it was something to do with the story, he was sure, but couldn't now get hold of it. He'd intended to replace the folder where he'd found it, before Mum noticed it was missing – why hadn't he sneaked it back down when he'd finished reading?

In the shower, he found himself remembering details: the cry of the buzzard, the cackle of grouse, the shapes in the mist. Yes, *that* was what he'd been dreaming; he'd been blundering about on the hillside, stumbling, unable to find his way through boulders and tussocks of grass, all the time knowing he must get down to safety, never let himself sit down and rest. And ahead of him, all the time, had been the ghost-grey shape of the dog. Leading him to safety, or farther away from it?

It was a bit like a fairy tale, the way it was written, but what if it were true? Why would Wil write a story like that, otherwise – and if it were made-up, why would the boy be called Tommy *Jones*? Could Wil have written the story of his own little boy, who'd wandered off and died? The bit about the ghost dog couldn't be true; but maybe Wil wanted to think that Tommy hadn't been alone, that he'd had warm, friendly company when he fell asleep for the last time. That could be his reason for writing it at all: making up a better version, turning the stark facts into a fairy story, to make himself feel better. Because if Tommy, aged only five, had wandered off and got lost on the mountain, it had to be his father's fault.

Matt pulled on jeans, sweatshirt and trainers, frowning. It still didn't add up. If Tommy had been Wil's little boy, then who was Owen? And why did Wil have Martin's photo in his cottage, if it *was* Martin? The boy in the photograph, at any rate, wasn't five years old; more like twelve, so he definitely couldn't be Tommy. Wouldn't you expect Wil to have Tommy's picture some- where? But then there might be other photos in the front room or bedroom . . . For a moment he considered trying to get inside the cottage again, making up some excuse to have a good look round. Then he remembered he'd decided never to go there again.

'Matty!' yelled Dad, up the stairs. 'I'm doing you some toast. Get a move on!'

Matt slipped the beige folder inside *Skateboard* magazine and went down. Waiting for the toast to pop up, he glanced in at the shop, saw that Mum was busy with a customer by the History shelf, and slipped the folder back where he'd found it, on top of the box.

Down in the cellar, he mixed whitewash in a bucket, and sloshed it on the walls with a big brush, watching all the grimy marks, paint scrapes and chipped bits of plaster disappear under smooth whiteness. Instantly, the place was cleaner and brighter. 'It'll need a second coat,' Dad said, standing back to admire the result, 'but it dries quickly, this stuff. Then I'll put shelves all along this back wall. Can you nip up and get the measuring tape? I think it's on the shop counter.'

Matt climbed the echoey cellar steps and went through to the shop. As he entered, the front doorbell jingled, and he stopped dead, seeing who was coming in. *Wil!* Matt's head reeled. Each time Wil came here, it seemed that thinking about him had magicked him out of the air.

'Hello, Mr Jones!' Mum exclaimed; she was on her knees, sorting Biography. Wil might have been the person she hoped to see above all others. She stood up, dusting off her hands against her jeans.

'Morning, Mrs Lanchester.' Wil lifted his peaked cap.

Matt ducked back behind the doorframe. This was getting to be a habit, eavesdropping. This time, he gave himself the excuse that he was protecting Mum. She shouldn't be left alone with a man who'd killed someone.

Wil sounded hesitant. 'Sorry to bother you again—'

'No, you're welcome, any time!' Mum told him. 'I've been looking up some of those books you brought, but I've got more websites to check—'

'It's not those I've come about,' said Wil. 'Fact is, I made a mistake. Brought something I didn't mean to. Maybe you saw it – brown folder, with some typed pages in it.'

'Oh yes, I know.' Mum's voice moved nearer. 'I thought perhaps you hadn't meant to bring that. Don't worry, it's quite safe here.'

Just in time!

Mum reached for the folder and handed it over; Wil clutched it to his chest, thanked her and thanked her again, his voice wavery with relief. 'Thank God! Began to think I'd put it out with the rubbish, see – searched and searched for it last night. Don't know how I'd have told Gwynnie, if I'd thrown out her story – oh, I can't thank you enough, Mrs Lanchester.'

'No trouble,' said Mum. 'Gwynnie? Is that your wife – Mrs Jones? And she writes stories – how wonderful!'

'Always has – loves writing stories, and telling them,' Wil said. He sounded proud now. 'Never tried to get them published. Never wanted any of that malarkey. Writes them for herself, she says, and anyone who wants to read them. What with the convalescing, she thought she'd read them over, all her old ones. Maybe write some more.'

'Oh, is Mrs Jones at home now?' Mum asked politely. 'You must be so pleased.'

'This afternoon,' Wil said. 'I'm bringing her home later. It's not been like home without her.'

Mum made a sympathetic sound, and said, 'I hope things'll soon be back to normal, then.'

Matt, pressed against the wall and hardly breathing, wondered if Wil would tell Gwynnie about the dead chicken, or whether she'd see it for herself on the compost heap. Or maybe they'd bury it together in the orchard, giving it a solemn funeral, with a bunch of primroses laid on the fresh grave. No, how daft was that? Wil had a rifle, he shot things – death and killing must be part of his life.

He wished Wil would hurry up and go. Each time he came here, Matt was afraid he'd say something to Mum, something like 'That boy of yours has been making a nuisance of himself. Little vandal, he is.' To say that Mum would be cross would be putting it mildly. But it had never happened: for some reason, Wil never seemed to connect the Matt he'd met in the shop with the boy who'd been appearing at his cottage. They must be in two separate bits of his mind, never meeting.

'That's all done, then, with the books,' Wil said. 'I've finished the clear-out now.'

'I'm very pleased you gave me first look at them,' said Mum. 'And I'll get back to you about the special ones, soon as I can. I've been looking up *The Owl Service* – it might be worth a hundred and fifty, even two hundred pounds – it's certainly collectable.'

'Two hundred pounds?' Wil repeated, bewildered. 'And I might have put it out with the rubbish!'

Mum gave a small shudder. 'I'm very glad you didn't! Oh – you haven't given me your phone number, have you?' She reached for a pencil and pad, wrote down the number Wil gave her, then repeated it aloud.

One thing Matt was good at remembering was numbers. He memorized Wil's, and recited it to himself silently.

'I'll ring you, soon as I find anything out,' Mum said again. 'I must say, Mr Jones, your children were very lucky to have such fantastic books – but now other people can read them. Do they still live in the area, your children?'

Wil made a throaty sound that might or might not have been a word. Then he mumbled, 'The one boy, we had.' Matt heard that, quite distinctly.

Had?

He hoped Mum would ask more, but Wil was already moving towards the door, clutching the folder. 'Well, I'll be getting back. Thanks again.'

Matt slipped away, back to the cellar. Dad looked exasperated, seeing him empty-handed. 'Well, where's the tape?'

Oops! He'd forgotten what he went up for. He found Mum humming happily to herself, looking things up on the Internet; she didn't even notice as he grabbed the measuring tape and went back down.

So it was *Gwynnie* who'd written that story! How much did that change things? Matt frowned to himself, stirring whitewash with a stick. Not much, really: Gwynnie had written it, but it was still the story of Tommy Jones, her son and Wil's. The story was the same. *The one boy, we had.* Tommy, it must be! *Had* – because they'd lost him, in such a tragic, careless way. No wonder Wil felt guilty! He was surely to blame, not only for Martin's death, but for Tommy's as well. How awful was that? Not the sort of thing you could easily forget.

But, Matt puzzled, dunking his brush into the bucket and lifting it out, dripping, where did that leave Owen? Wil's brother, maybe? Or what if *Wil's* name was really Owen? Would that explain it? Perhaps he'd changed it after the death of Martin – trying to pretend he wasn't the killer? But in a place like this, people would know. You'd have to move right away, change everything, or it wouldn't fool anyone. Round and round his thoughts went, tangling themselves, forming new knots and muddles.

Later, when he and Dad had finished whitewashing and rinsed the brushes, Mum called him into the shop. There were no customers. She tidied away a few odds and ends from the counter, and arranged leaflets in neat piles. The slight awkwardness of her manner sent out warning signals. Maybe Wil had said something after all – remembered, and come back.

But Mum started off on a different tack.

'That boy Tim you go around with – Tig, you call him. You get on all right with him, don't you?'

'He's OK.' This wasn't what Matt had expected. 'He's a good mate.'

'There's that other boy, Rob, isn't there? Where d'you go to, the three of you?'

'Nowhere much.' Matt shuffled a foot on the carpet. 'Kick a ball about, go out on the bikes. Hang out. What's wrong with that?' He sounded stroppier than he meant to. 'What, has Fen said something?'

'No – why would she?' Mum looked at him closely; he felt himself going red, remembering the conversation he'd overheard with Dad. If they stopped him from going out on his bike, then what? What if he couldn't go around with Tig and Robbo any more? – they'd call him a wimp, a mummy's boy. But not having the freedom to go where he liked would be far worse than that.

'I'm going out,' he told her, ignoring her protest that it was nearly time for lunch.

Matt went out to the side shed where his bike was kept. It wasn't nice, being at odds with Mum like this; he didn't like the way it made him feel inside. But he couldn't backtrack. He wondered what she'd heard about Tig – if not from Fen, then from someone else. Her drama group, perhaps; people gossiped in a little place like this. Tig was trouble, he'd known that instinctively – so why did he feel that Tig deserved his loyalty? The thing was, Tig had a weird kind of power. Where it came from, this ability to make other people feel stupid, or deeply uncool, Matt had no idea; but all Tig needed to do was to let his eyes roll upwards, or puff out his breath, or give the smallest hint of that lopsided smile, and others would follow.

He pushed the bike out to the street and pedalled off, not really knowing where he was heading. Not to Wil's, that was for sure – he'd seen enough of that dismal place. He'd thought he never wanted to see Martin's cross again, but nevertheless found himself turning in that direction, away from town. It had been raining, and the tyres sang along the wet surface; the hedgerows were dense, dripping, bursting with new growth. Almost of its own accord, his bike stopped by Martin's tree; he was looking at it before he was fully aware of where he was. With the new leaves almost luminous green in the hedgerow, the bareness of the dead tree was all the more noticeable. Matt wondered, fancifully, if it had died when Martin did, in sympathy.

His attention was caught by the pale brightness of primroses against the grass: a thick bunch of them, held in a rubber band, laid on the ground. Someone had been here; someone who remembered Martin. Martin's parents? He hadn't asked Tig who they were, but Hay was a small town where people knew each other. That meant they must know Wil – must see him as he came into town, and went about his business. Did they speak to each other? Or cross the pavement to avoid having to look at him?

Matt stood looking, at the initials M.L. that still sent a shiver down his back whenever he saw them. How often did they come, Martin's parents, come and stand at the place where their son had died, and leave fresh flowers? Wouldn't they prefer to remember him some other way, by going to his grave, or the places he liked?

He pushed on. This place sent a funny prickling feeling through him, all the way to his toes and his fingers. At least this time there was no sense of Martin waiting for him, watching to see what he'd do. He didn't know whether he was glad or sorry about that. He was beginning to expect Martin's presence, almost to look for him; he'd become used to him, so that it hardly seemed strange any more. But it was Martin who chose when to appear and when to be elusive, and Matt couldn't follow him: couldn't cross the great dividing line that separated them.

Instead of taking the turn up towards Dan-y-fforest, he went straight ahead, up the lane that rounded a bend, then rose steeply between high hedges. A sheep pasture was ahead and to the right, and he could hear urgent baa-ing – sheep and lambs, the ewes' voices almost comically deep, the lambs' high and anxious. Something was happening. The sheep were massed tightly, bunching in a corner of the field. Their ears were alert, all pointing the same way.

Pushing uphill, in low gear, Matt saw a dog moving towards them, and a man walking slowly behind. He heard the whistle of command, saw the dog, a black-and-white collie, lie down on the grass, then move on, herding the flock tight by the hedge. Good, that was, the man and the dog working together, skilled and sure: always watching, always seeing exactly how the sheep would react, and how to stop them from panicking and running all over the field. The man blew a high, shrill note on his whistle and the dog crept forward, watchful, moving the sheep forward. They were heading for a gateway, moving the ewes and lambs from one field to another. It wasn't a big flock, maybe twenty ewes, but they were massed together almost as one creature, until three or four of the laggards tried to break away at the fence and go in a different direction, like spray breaking from a wave. At once the dog was there, flanking and turning them, and the flock was one again, surging towards the gateway. The leaders were through; they ran wide and free, the ewes still alert to the dog, while their lambs pressed close. Some of the bolder lambs broke away and cavorted around the fresh pasture, making funny stilt-like leaps.

The man walked up and closed the gate, took the whistle from his lips and called the dog to him. It was Wil, and the dog was Jacko. They were a team.

ELEVEN

Persuasion

Wednesday, the day of the mountain walk; Matt was up early, looking out of his attic window. The sky was grey and overcast, but it wasn't raining. That looked hopeful. Adam said they'd wait for a better day if the weather was really bad.

Mum went out early, to the shops. Her way of dealing with arguments, like the one about Tig, was to pretend they hadn't happened; she wasn't like some people's mums, who could go all stern and huffy for days on end when things went wrong. With her first Bed and Breakfast guests due to arrive, she'd been double-checking everything, cleaning toilets that were already gleaming, and dusting speckless furniture.

While Matt ate his cereal, she unpacked her shopping bags. 'Brown sauce!' she exclaimed, clapping a hand to her forehead. 'Oh no, I forgot the brown sauce!'

'Can't they make do with tomato?' Dad said, pouring coffee.

Mum shook her head emphatically. *'Make do? Our guests? That's* not the way to get my Tourist Board stars, is it? No, I ought to have both. Matt, you couldn't nip down and get some, could you?' She looked at her watch. 'You'll have time, before the twins get here. I'll do your packed lunch while you're gone. And maybe I should have more kinds of jam – could you get a jar of blackcurrant?'

Matt took the five-pound note she gave him and jogged down to the Spar shop. Going in, he almost bumped into Tig, who was paying for a Coke and a bar of chocolate.

'Hi,' Matt said, uneasily.

Tig looked at him without smiling. 'Where'd you get to, yesterday?'

'Had to help my dad.'

'We waited, me and Robbo. Waited half an hour. You could've told us.'

'Forgot, didn't I?' Matt tried to sound offhand; he headed past, towards the shelves.

Tig blocked his way. 'Not so fast. How about it, then?'

'How about what?' Matt bluffed.

'You know.' Tig lowered his voice. 'Going up Dan-y-fforest.'

'Can't,' Matt told him. 'Doing something else today. Anyway, I've changed my mind.'

'Oh, you've changed your mind, have you?' Tig echoed, putting on a prissy voice. 'Mummy and Daddy don't like you playing with nasty rough boys, is that it?'

This was uncomfortably close to the truth. 'You go, if you want,' said Matt. 'Leave me out of it.'

'Oh, but I can't.' Tig had managed to manoeuvre Matt with his back against the fruit and veg, his tallness blocking Matt from the view of anyone in the shop; he'd created a little huddle of privacy for the two of them. 'Can't do it without you, can I? How's it going to work if you don't join in?'

'Don't know what you mean.' Matt tried to slip past him, but Tig stepped closer, penning him in.

'Yes, you do. This is what. We all go up there, but only you go in.'

'What for?'

'Pretend to be Martin,' Tig said. 'That'll really send him mental.'

Matt glanced away. 'No! I'm not doing it.'

'Yes, you are.' Tig looked at him steadily. 'Because if you don't, something worse'll happen. Up at Wil's. I promise you.'

'What d'you mean? What sort of thing?' Matt was almost trembling, determined not to let Tig

111

see. He tried to sound hard. 'Why've you got it in for him, anyway?'

'Look,' said Tig, in a quiet, soothing voice. 'I know things you don't know. Trust me. I'll tell you later.'

In that moment, held by Tig's compelling gaze, Matt felt that he could and should trust him. And beyond Tig, there was Martin; always in the shadows of Matt's mind, watching, wanting him to find out. Wasn't Martin nudging him, as well as Tig?

'I can't, not today,' Matt stalled. 'I'm going out all day. How about tomorrow?'

Tig moved back fractionally; his mouth made the faintest twitch towards a smile.

'Right, sorted. Ten o'clock, car park?'

Left to himself, Matt wandered along the shelves, unable for a few moments to remember what he'd come for. Brown sauce. Right. Blackcurrant jam. The day already seemed spoiled, the day he'd been looking forward to.

TWELVE

Obelisk

Why did I tell Tig I'd go? Matt's thoughts were going round and round in a spiral. *What am I playing at?*

They were marching up a stony track from a reservoir, Adam, the twins and Matt. The twins' father had driven them to the starting point, and would pick them up later from the Storey Arms, on the other side of the mountain. A brisk wind was gusting, the sky was grey, but with sunlight almost breaking through. If only it wasn't for the reproachful thoughts in Matt's head, repeating themselves with every stride! He wanted to enjoy the outing, forget all about Tig and Wil and Martin for once, not worry about them all the way up Pen-y-Fan and down again.

The slopes of the mountain stretched away high to their left, the top invisible in mist.

'Up there, we're going.' Sian pointed dramatically. 'Up there in the cloud!'

She was as lively as a goat kid, skipping over rocks, running ahead then doubling back, until Adam told her to stop. 'You've got to pace yourself on a walk like this. You'll run out of energy, and don't expect a piggyback from me if you do!'

'Adam's very strict,' Sian warned Matt.

Adam was. Although his height and long legs would have let him stride much faster, he kept to a steady pace. He made sure everyone had water and chocolate when they paused for a break; when the mist turned to light rain, he stopped again and told them to put on their waterproofs.

'It'll be too hot,' Bryn grumbled, but Adam told him, 'It's daft to get damp, *then* put on your wet gear. Just do it.'

Before they moved off again, he showed Matt the route; his map was in a waterproof case slung round his neck. 'It's very straightforward. We can't get lost.'

'Famous last words,' Bryn said.

'No, we can't. This is the main path, and anyway I've got my compass.'

'You'd never get lost with Ad,' Sian told Matt. 'As long as he's got his map and compass he can find his way to a single rock in the middle of nowhere, *and* in the dark.'

'*And* know exactly how long it'll take to walk there,' Bryn added.

'Well, it's not too difficult when you've practised a bit,' Adam said modestly. 'It's only maths.'

'*Only* maths!' It was Matt's worst subject.

Maths apart, though, he decided that he wanted to be like Adam: fit, and capable, and the sort of bloke no one could help liking. Adam told him a bit more about the leadership course he was doing in North Wales; when he'd qualified, he'd be able to take groups on expeditions, not only walking but also caving and canoeing, and teach mountain and survival skills. 'So I'll be able to do this sort of thing, and call it work!'

They were gaining height now, the gradient pulling at the backs of Matt's legs. Out of the mist came three soldiers in combat gear, carrying heavy packs; they were walking together but not speaking, and only one of them managed a brief 'Hello' as they passed. Matt saw that they were only teenage boys, Adam's age or younger.

'They do army training up here,' Adam told Matt. 'You often see groups of squaddies. Sometimes one on his own.'

'Or *her* own,' said Sian. 'You get girls in the army as well, you know.'

'I wouldn't fancy slogging all the way up with one of those big packs.' Bryn eased the small rucksack off his shoulders. 'Mine weighs enough.'

'That's cos you've got twice as much lunch as anyone else,' Sian teased.

Soon, as the path became much steeper, Matt was out of breath. He wasn't as fit as the twins, who were used to hill-walking, but was desperate not to drop behind. Adam kept glancing round, making sure they were all together, and pausing to look at his map. Catching up with Sian, Matt was pleased to notice that she too was puffing, and had stopped for a breather. A few moments, and they were ready to carry on.

'What you have to do,' Sian said, 'is not stop till you've climbed, say, forty steps up. Then it's a kind of reward to stop and look round, and see how much higher you've come.'

Their world had both shrunk and expanded. In the mist, Matt could see only a few metres ahead: the broad path, worn bare by countless boots; the tough grass on each side, short-nibbled by sheep, and scattered here and there with the dark pellets of their droppings. There were boulders to the left, but on the right was a steep drop that fell away out of sight. Yet Matt was aware of space and hugeness: the air was cool against his face, and his eyelashes beaded with moisture, from walking through cloud. Although he couldn't see the mountaintops he knew that the summits were pushing into the sky, and that the towns and villages far below, and the roads threading the valleys, were dwarfed by the hulking hills.

'We won't see much from the top,' Adam said, disappointed.

The path grew even steeper, reaching a sort of rocky platform and the triangulation point. Sian, finding a new burst of energy, sprinted ahead and stood there triumphant. As the others joined her, the mist drifted away, leaving a clear patch in which Matt could see how steeply the ground was scooped away from the edge. In the valley below, he saw green fields dotted with sheep, and someone walking, a tiny figure against a hedge. Matt had the silly idea that if he ran and jumped off the cliff, he'd float like a dandelion clock, drifting slowly down to the valley.

The feeling came into his mind that he'd stood here before, looking down at the drop, at the swooping cliff. Hadn't he? Or only dreamed it? No – he fished around in his memory – he'd *read* it—

. . . the land was scooped away, falling and falling down sheer cliffs that made him dizzy to look at them, as if a giant had taken an enormous spoon, the most enormous spoon imaginable, and sliced away a huge mouthful of mountain . . .

It exactly described what Matt saw below him. A tingle shivered through him as he realised that he was standing on top of the mountain Tommy

Jones and his father had seen as they walked to Tommy's grandfather's farm. He couldn't be far from where Tommy Jones had died.

'Is that our way down?' he asked, looking at the drop.

Adam smiled. 'That's the *quick* way down – but I'd prefer to get there in one piece, if it's all the same to you. No, we'll go this way'—he indicated with a flung arm—'down to the obelisk.'

'Obelisk, Obelisk,' Sian chanted.

'What's an obbalisk?' Matt asked, wondering if he ought to know.

'It's a *mountain monster*!' Sian came at him with eyes wide and fingers stretched like claws. 'Haven't you ever seen one? It's a cross between a hobbit and a dinosaur, with hairy feet and a long scaly tail – it hobbles along, and it'th got no teeth, that'th why it talkth like thith!'

'She's gone mountain-mad.' Adam shook his head, mock-sadly. 'The altitude's gone to her head, that's what does it. She'll get back to normal, eventually.'

'And it knows,' Sian went on, making her voice deep and ominous, 'that lots of people don't believe in it, so they can't see it, even though it makes a squelching noise when it hobbles – and it sneaks up behind them, and gobbles them up, every bit of them except their boots and the clips on their rucksack. Not many people know this, but it's attracted by *peanut butter sandwiches*. Especially,' she added, looking sternly at Bryn, 'peanut butter with *redcurrant jelly*. So we'd better eat ours before we get down there.'

'OK, we'll have lunch here,' Adam said, looking at his watch, 'only put your sweatshirts on, or you'll get cold. An obelisk,' he told Matt, 'is a sort of memorial.'

'A memorial to all the victims of the mountain monster,' Sian added. 'More than anyone knows how to count. You can tell by all the rucksack clips scattered around.'

'I'll tell you about it when we're there.' Adam settled himself on a rock, and pulled out a flask from his pack. 'That's if Sian's monster doesn't pounce on us first.'

Bryn really *had* got peanut-butter-and-redcurrant-jelly sandwiches. 'Want one?' He offered his lunchbox to Matt. 'They're delishioso!'

Matt, who thought it sounded revolting, tried a mouthful and had to agree.

'He has them nearly every day at school, can you believe?' Sian said, talking with her mouth full. 'PB and J, we call them.'

A few other walkers came to join them on the summit, and more could be seen on Corn Dhu, close by. It was too cold to stay long, and soon they were on their feet again, ready to move on.

Sian's daftness about the obelisk monster had driven away the dreamlike feeling Matt had of walking in Tommy Jones's footsteps, but they all fell silent as they walked down a slope away from the summit, with the big cliff falling away to the right. The mist had crept up again, shrouding everything in a strange, pearly light, and muffling the sound. Adam never faltered, but Matt began to understand how easy it would be, up here, to lose all sense of direction and blunder off the wrong way, or even over the steep edge they were following so closely. A bird called, high and mewing, invisible in cloud.

'Here we are,' Adam said. A shape loomed up: Matt could have thought it was a tall, cloaked figure, guarding the place. Then he saw that it was a pillar of stone, marking one end of a depression in the ground. This hollow, level but not deep, made Matt imagine a flying saucer landing there, flattening the earth, then taking off again.

'That's the obelisk,' Bryn told Matt. 'The Tommy Jones Obelisk.'

'Tommy Jones?' Matt echoed.

'You said you'd tell him, Ad.' Sian pulled off her pack and settled herself on the grassy edge of the hollow.

'Tommy Jones?' Matt repeated. 'The boy who wandered off and died?'

'Oh, you've heard the story?' Adam said. 'Well, it's quite well-known.'

'Is it?' Matt was surprised. 'I thought – I mean, I thought Tommy Jones was Wil's son – I didn't know it was a famous story.'

'Wil?'

'Wil Jones,' Matt said. What had made him mention Wil, when he wanted to forget about him? 'He lives in a cottage up at Dan-y-fforest.'

Adam gave him a puzzled look. 'No, no. I know who you mean. But Tommy Jones was a lot longer ago. More than a hundred years.' He gestured towards the stone pillar. 'There's a book about him – I've got it at home.'

'You're in Wales, Matt,' Bryn said, taking advantage of the halt to eat another sandwich. 'You don't have to go far to meet someone called Jones.'

Baffled, Matt dumped his pack; he went to the obelisk to read the carved letters:

This obelisk marks the spot where the body of TOMMY JONES, aged five, was found. He lost his way between Cwmllwch Farm and the Login, on the night of August 4th 1900. After an anxious search of twenty-nine days his remains were discovered Sept 2.

'Are we sitting comfortably?' Sian said, perched on her turf seat. 'Come on, Ad.'

They all sat in a row, feet in the dip.

'Well,' Adam began, 'Tommy Jones was heading for his grandfather's farm, down in the valley there, with his dad. It was an August night, and they'd already walked a long way from the train to get here, and there was a bit of a mis-understanding, and Tommy ended up walking on his own, for the last bit. It wasn't far – look.' He showed Matt on the map. 'From here, to this farm here, along the stream. No one knows why, but he wandered right off course – took the wrong path altogether, on to the hillside. In the mist and the wet that was dangerous, even in August. See, you've only got to think how cold and wet it'd be now, if you didn't have the right gear. He didn't. And nothing to eat – you'd get chilled in no time. Well, this is where he died, poor boy. We've come a fair way down from the top, now, but if you came *up*, from the valley, it'd feel like quite a climb – so why he kept going, no one can say. Course, everyone was frantic, when he didn't show up, and the first thing they thought was he'd fallen in the river down there. Then they searched all the farm buildings and the fields, and then they must have started thinking he'd been murdered or kidnapped. It was nearly a month later when they found him, right where we are now. But everyone remembers Tommy Jones when they come here,' Adam finished, indicating the obelisk. 'Sometimes you see a big group of walkers sat round in a circle here, everyone sad for Tommy Jones.'

'And that's what we always do,' Sian said, serious now, with no more mountain monster tales. 'We think about Tommy Jones, so he won't feel so lonely.'

Matt thought. He thought of Tommy's small body, curled in sleep; he'd seen it so clearly while reading the story that it seemed part of his own memory. And he thought of Gwilym, the ghost dog, haunting this place; forever sad, forever mourning his own failure. He imagined Gwilym howling into the mist, answered by the cry of the buzzard.

There had been no Gwilym in Adam's story; no ghost-dog for a companion. Here, though, in the place of Tommy's death, it seemed easy to believe. But Tommy wasn't Wil's and Gwynnie's son, after all; Gwynnie had only written down her own version of a story lots of people knew. Matt felt disappointed that his theory had fallen to bits. Still, the Tommy Jones story – now that he'd been to the exact place, had seen its wild beauty and its dangers – was vivid in his mind.

'Can I borrow that book?' he asked Adam.

Adam nodded. 'Sure – remind me when we get home. Everyone OK? Finished meditating? We'll get on down to the Storey Arms – Dad'll be there soon.'

As they rejoined the broad main path and continued down, Matt turned to look back. It wouldn't take much imagination to see the grey shape of Gwilym, part of the mist that enclosed that lonely place, almost sealing it off from the world below: Gwilym, keeping his promise for all eternity.

THIRTEEN

Martin Lloyd

As Adam was meeting friends in Hay for the evening, he gave Matt a lift home; he parked near the craft centre and they walked together as far as Kilvert's Hotel. From here, Adam was heading for the pub in the next street, Matt turning right for home.

'Thanks for today – it was great,' Matt was saying, when he saw that Adam's attention was caught by someone coming towards them, along Bear Street. It was a boy of about Adam's age, tall, skinny, in jeans and a leather jacket. He had a slouching walk, hands in pockets.

Adam nodded to him, and said, 'Luke.' It wasn't really a hello, just a sign of recognition. And he didn't smile, which was unusual, as Adam was usually a smiley sort of person.

The other boy only grunted in reply, barely glancing at Adam. Not slowing his pace, he turned towards the Wheatsheaf, where Adam was going.

His nose was long and bony, his face thin. He reminded Matt of someone.

'Is that one of the people you're meeting?' he asked.

'No,' Adam said curtly. 'He was in my year at school, but I wouldn't call him a friend. Luke's got a younger brother in your form at school. You know – Tig?'

Of course. *That* was who. Tig had mentioned his brother a few times; he'd been away from home for some reason. Since Luke and Adam apparently disliked each other, Matt didn't want to let on that he was friends with Tig. Well, *was* he?

'Bye, then.' Adam raised a hand in farewell, and Matt walked the short distance home. His legs were aching from the climb, and had already stiffened up a bit during the drive back.

Mum's bed and breakfast guests had arrived, a man and a woman of about Matt's grandparents' age, and Mum was in the hallway telling them where they could get an evening meal. It felt odd having strangers at home; the house didn't quite seem to be their own any more. Mum had asked him to remember not to go racketing down the stairs, or leave stuff cluttering the hall, or play his music too loudly. Still, at least the guests would have brown sauce at breakfast. *Brown sauce* – uncomfortably, Matt's thoughts flicked back to the shop, standing by the fruit and veg, and Tig fixing him with that stare he did, that made it impossible to break the contact.

With a feeling of heaviness settling over him, Matt remembered his promise to go to Wil's tomorrow. If he ducked out of it, *something worse'll happen* – Matt didn't know what Tig meant by that, and didn't want to find out, but that was the hold Tig had over him. It felt like waiting to have a tooth filled – it had to happen, and be got over with. *Next* time he'd say no. Definitely.

Later, in bed, he took out the book Adam had lent him, *The Story of Tommy Jones*. It was more pamphlet than book, but unlike Gwynnie's typescript it was properly printed and illustrated, with a map and a photograph of the Obelisk. It didn't take long to read. The story was more or less as Adam had told it, with no mention of the dog Gwilym, or the cries of the buzzard and the red grouse.

Reaching the end, Matt flicked back to the beginning, and his eyes blurred in astonishment. A name was written in biro inside the front cover, and not just any name – the words *Martin Lloyd* jumped out at him, then jumbled and whirled into nonsense. He had to blink, look again, and take in the name twice more before he could be sure he was seeing straight. *Martin Lloyd* – M.L.! Martin's name, written in – presumably – his own handwriting!

Matt's hands fumbled at the pages; the book dropped to the floor. He reached down for it, and opened it to check yet again. He could easily believe that Martin had crept into the room, and was breathing over his shoulder.

How had Adam got a book that belonged to Martin?

Matt flung himself on his bed and gazed at the ceiling, trying to sort things into some sort of logic. Names and faces spiralled round him in a teasing dance: Martin, Tommy Jones, and now *Adam.*

So Martin had read the Tommy Jones story – had read these same pages, the story of another lost boy . . . and now Adam had Martin's book . . .

'Martin?' Matt said aloud. '*You* know. Come on – this is doing my head in!'

But Martin wouldn't be summoned. There was only one person Matt could ask. He thought of creeping downstairs to the phone, but didn't want Mum or Dad to hear. His mobile was what he needed, but he'd run out of credit.

Fen was in her room; he'd heard her moving about. He crossed the landing and knocked. He could hear music inside, the floopy Corrs stuff she liked, all violins and voices and Irish jigging.

'Come in,' Fen called, in a flat-sounding voice.

He expected her to be at the desk, but instead she was lying on her bed, fully dressed. She might even have been asleep. Perkins, a long tabby shape, was stretched out beside her, clenching his claws on the duvet in catty contentment.

'What's up?'

'I'm OK,' she said dully.

He turned to her desk. Books and folders were stacked neatly. All closed.

'Have you finished it all?'

'No. Hardly started.'

Matt looked at her uneasily. If she'd been some *normal* girl, he'd have thought that lying on a bed listening to music was just what girls did. But not Fen. And not only was she not working; she looked thoroughly miserable about it, too.

'Why don't you *do* the work, then, if you're so worried?'

'I can't!' Her voice was edged with panic. 'I just can't. It's like my brain's seized up or something. I just can't *do* any more. I sit there and stare at my books and the words don't

129

even make sense.' She flung out an arm, disturbing the cat, who withdrew offended to wash his paws at the end of her bed.

'Well, what d'you expect?' said Matt. 'Give yourself a break.'

'I'm *having* a break!' Fen glared at him. 'What's it look like?'

'No, I mean go out with your friends and do stuff. Have some fun.'

Fen gave him a withering look, as if *fun* couldn't possibly have anything to do with her. 'What d'you want, anyway?'

'Can I borrow your mobile? Mine's out of credit.'

'If you must.' She nodded towards her bedside table. 'Only if it's quick, though. I need a top-up too.'

Matt went back to his own room and closed the door, then dialled the twins' number, which was written on a scrap of paper pinned to his corkboard. *Dumbo!* he told himself, as soon as he heard the ringtone; Adam wasn't there, was he? But before he'd rung off, Bryn answered. 'Ty Mawr Cottage.'

'Bryn, it's Matt.'

'Hi!' Bryn didn't seem surprised.

'You know that book Adam lent me? The Tommy Jones book? I've been reading it. It's got – it's got a name written in it.'

'Yeah, and?'

'Martin Lloyd, it says. Why's Adam got Martin's book?'

'Martin Lloyd,' Bryn repeated. 'Oh, right. He used to be Ad's best friend. He got killed, in an accident. Years and years ago, but Ad still talks about it sometimes. Anyway, it was good today, wasn't it? Me and Sian are going to ask Ad to take us down the Nedd Gorge next time – there's brill waterfalls there. You can go right round behind, there's sort of caves. Want to come?'

'You bet,' said Matt.

'Sunday or Monday, most likely. I'll ring you.'

Matt rang off, and sat thinking. So Adam knew about Wil – Wil had killed his best friend! *I know who you mean* was all Adam had said, when Matt mentioned Wil's name; but he'd looked as if he could have said more. Matt had almost raised the subject in the car on the way back, but then hadn't. What more could Adam have told him?

Well, there was no way of finding out now. Matt took Fen's mobile back to her. Perkins was sitting up on the duvet, still vigorously washing himself, but Fen hadn't moved; she lay quite still.

'Are you ill, or what?' he asked, and his

voice came out on tiptoe.

'No, I'm *not*,' Fen snapped back.

'Why don't you go down and watch TV or something?'

'Leave me alone, for God's sake! And put my phone back over there. I hope you've left it switched on.'

She wasn't usually bad-tempered, either. Matt shut the door and left her to it; but back in his own room he found himself wondering: *What if she's seriously cracking up? Like Wil?* There seemed to be a lot of it about. You took it for granted that your brain carried on with its normal stuff – woke up, went to sleep, thought its thoughts and dreamed its dreams – but what if it went wrong, like a radio that couldn't be tuned in, and you only got fizzing and hissing? How would you *know*, since inside your own head was the only place you could be? And what if it started picking up strange vibrations – the way his own brain was letting in the Martin weirdness? He didn't even want to think about that.

So what should he do about Fen? Yes, he'd promised; but what if she really did need help, or at least someone to take notice? Besides, the promise had been to keep quiet about her over-working. Her *not* working was different, and odder.

And next there was tomorrow, and Tig.

Wearied by all the problems life was throwing at him, he crawled back into bed, turned off his lamp and tugged the duvet up around his ears.

FOURTEEN

Gwynnie

'Go on.' Tig prodded Matt in the back. 'Be Martin. Tell him you're never going away. Tell him you'll never forget, and neither will he.'

Robbo giggled.

'This is stupid,' Matt grumped. 'And what's the point?'

Tig didn't answer, but shared a quick secretive glance with Rob.

'What'll you two be doing, while I'm in there?' said Matt, one hand on the gate.

'Just waiting!' Tig said, his face innocent. 'Hide in the bushes, like last time. We want to hear all about it when you come out. Exactly what he says. What he does.'

'He'll go mental,' Rob said, with relish.

'Yeah, great. And he's got a gun. I suppose you're hoping he'll use it on me,' Matt retorted.

The three bikes were left in the gateway, down the lane. They had sneaked up close to Wil's gate, from where Matt saw a plume of smoke rising from the cottage chimney, and Wil's van parked in its usual place. Matt had the feeling that they ought to be wearing army combat gear like the cadets he'd seen on Pen-y-Fan, their faces smeared with blackened cork. It was a game to Robbo, more than a game to Tig. There was a sort of cold determination about Tig that made Matt fearful.

Wil was two quite separate people, that was the problem. He was the gruff old man who came to Mum's bookshop, and was grateful for her help; he was Gwynnie's husband, and Jacko's master. But he was also the drunk driver who'd knocked Martin off his bike and left him dying. Matt might have found it hard to believe that, if Wil himself hadn't admitted it.

Martin was Adam's best friend, he reminded himself. *And Wil killed him. Wil's alive, and Martin isn't. That can't be right.*

The shiver that came over him, warm and cold at once, alerted him to Martin's presence behind him, urging him to go in. *OK, then, I suppose I'll have to,* Matt thought. *Might as well get it over with.*

How to get inside the cottage, that was the first challenge. Robbo probably would have made faces at the window and whooped; Tig would have waited to sneak in. Matt simply went to the door and knocked. While he waited, Robbo sprang up from behind the fence making a rude gesture, then ducked out of view. Jacko was already barking; he knew they were there.

Slow footsteps sounded; a bolt slid back inside the door. Wil stood there, at first frowning, then puzzled, then tentatively smiling. Last time, he'd chased Matt away, with threats – Matt could only count on him being too confused to remember.

'Do ra vor,' Wil said to the dog. Jacko gave a final *gruff,* and pushed his nose into Matt's hand; Wil peered more closely at him, then stepped back and held the door open wide. 'Come in, boy! I knew you'd be back! Gwynnie! Gwynnie, come and see who's here!'

Gwynnie.

Of course, Gwynnie was here now – actually here, not like last time, when Wil had only imagined she was.

Matt stepped inside. Wil led the way through to the second room, the one Matt hadn't seen before – the one Wil had cleared ready for Gwynnie, because she couldn't manage the stairs. There was a sofa bed, a rocking chair and a stool, a television, and a dog basket lined with a hairy blanket. The papered walls showed pale strips and the neat holes of Rawlplugs, where shelves had been taken down. This was where the books had been kept; there were still two shelves, above a new-looking cabinet. The room smelled of lavender and talcum powder.

Whenever Wil had mentioned Gwynnie, Matt had imagined a stooped old lady in a rocking chair (and there it was!). She'd have a hearing aid, and white hair in a bun. She'd wear a cardigan with handkerchieves bulging the pockets, a thick skirt and brown stockings, and furry slippers. She'd drink tea and knit and listen to the radio. Sometimes she'd sit at a desk to work at her stories, writing scratchily in fountain pen, with real ink. Her hands, though, would be so knuckly and twisted with arthritis that she couldn't write for long. Somewhere there'd be the antiquated typewriter she used for typing them up. Being in hospital had left her even weaker, barely able to rise from her chair. That would be Gwynnie.

The woman who came through from the kitchen, leaning on a stick, was nothing like that at all. She was quite old, but not nearly as ancient as Matt's imaginary Gwynnie. She wore black track pants, trainers, a zipped red sweatshirt and gold ear-studs; her grey hair was cut short and curly.

'Here he is, Gwyn!' Wil said, triumphant. 'Here's Owen!'

Owen?

Gwynnie lurched over and put a hand on his shoulder. 'Wil, this isn't Owen. This is not Owen. You know it isn't.'

Wil rubbed his eyes. 'Who is he, then?' His voice sounded small, like a little boy's.

'That's a very good question.' Gwynnie turned to Matt. 'And I'd like an answer. Your name is—?'

'Matt.'

'Matt—?'

'Matt Lanchester.' He wondered why he hadn't made something up – Tig would have – but Gwynnie seemed the sort of person who'd know instantly if he lied, and get the truth out of him.

'Lanchester?' She looked at him closely, then turned to Wil and said, 'Lanchester? Isn't that the name of the bookshop you've been going to, the new one in Lion Street?'

Wil looked confused. 'Is it?'

'That's what you told me last week. So, you're from there, are you, Matt? It's your mother who's been helping Wil with the books?'

'I – yes.' This felt safer.

'And you go around with the Jenkins boy,' Gwynnie stated. 'Tig, isn't it? No, don't look so surprised. I've got ears and eyes, and there's not much goes unnoticed in a small place like this. I'm not a great gossiper myself, but one thing about being in hospital, it gives you plenty of time to catch up on local chat. Now, you'd better tell me what all this is about.'

If only he could!

Gwynnie, using her stick to lower herself, settled in the rocking chair and looked at him expectantly; Wil stood by the door, perhaps thinking Matt would try to make a bolt for it.

Matt gazed desperately around the room.

'Let me guess,' Gwynnie offered. 'Those Jenkins boys've got a grudge against Wil, I know that. You're new here, and you can't be expected to know all this ancient history. I'd guess Tig Jenkins is getting you to do his dirty work for him, is that it? You don't look like a troublemaker – but let me tell you, *he* is.'

'I—'

'He knows Wil's been on his own here, past week or so, and he's taken advantage. I suppose he told you it would be a good joke to come here pretending to be Owen?'

Uh?

'No!' Matt protested.

Gwynnie glanced round. 'Wil, I think we could all do with a cup of tea.'

She had a way of saying things that didn't leave much choice. Wil, after giving her a doubtful look, shuffled obediently into the kitchen; Jacko padded after him. Gwynnie gestured to Matt to sit on the stool, then rounded on him again.

'Don't you think Wil's got enough to worry about? He's not good on his own, but you had to go making things worse? Is that your idea of fun, or do you do whatever the Jenkins boy tells you?'

Matt wriggled and looked away from her penetrating gaze.

'But I *didn't* pretend to be Owen,' he said. 'I don't even know who Owen is.'

Gwynnie looked at him hard. 'You didn't come here trying to fool Wil, and get him upset, is that what you're telling me?'

'No! I mean yes! I don't want to upset anyone. And I don't know anything about Owen.'

Gwynnie seemed to decide he was telling the truth. 'Oh, dear. It looks like Wil's done the muddling for himself.' She glanced towards the kitchen, then went on: 'Owen's our son. We haven't seen him for thirty-five years. You look a bit like him when he was a boy – only a bit, but enough to confuse Wil.'

'But—' Matt couldn't get his head round this. 'Thirty-five years?'

Gwynnie nodded. 'Course, he's not a boy now. But you do look like him.' She gave a sad smile, looking less formidable. 'Wil remembers him as he was, see. I'll show you his photograph in a minute.'

'I've seen it,' Matt said, realising – of course that was Owen in the picture next door, not Martin! 'What happened? How did you—' Lose him, he was about to say, but amended to: 'Why haven't you seen him?'

'He and Wil didn't get on. They always did, when Owen was a boy – but when Owen got to sixteen or so, that all changed. Wil's always been a farmer, always worked hard, kept sheep all his life and still does a bit of work for Lewis at the farm along there.'

'I know,' said Matt. 'I've seen him, with Jacko.'

Gwynnie nodded. 'Helps keep him going, that does. We used to keep our own sheep, owned a few more of these fields, back then before Wil retired. He always thought Owen would take over, it'd stay in the family. Owen, though, he wouldn't have any of it. Couldn't see a future in farming. Wanted to be in a rock band. They couldn't see eye to eye. Wil wanted Owen to settle down in a decent job and earn his living, but he only sneered at all that. Then one day, after a row – off he went to some music festival, and never came back. That's the last we know of him.'

'So what did you do? Did you get the police after him?'

'Oh yes! We told the police, we got in touch with Missing Persons, we did everything we could think of,' Gwynnie said. 'Wil's been looking for him ever since. But who knows where he might have gone? Made new friends at that festival, most like, set off for India or Thailand with a guitar and a rucksack the way people did back then – never came back, never told us where he'd gone, never so much as a phone call or postcard. Wil blamed himself, needless to say. It broke his heart. Well, and not only Wil's. And since Wil's been – well – wandering in his mind, it's all coming back.'

'But perhaps Owen *will*—' Matt tried. 'I mean, one day—'

'I don't think so. Not after all these years. He's got his own life, wherever he is. If only Wil would stop wishing – building up disappointment. This confusion only makes it worse. He still looks for him – never says so, but off he goes with Jacko, up to the top there, and he comes back sad, and I know he's been searching for Owen. Of course, it was Owen's right to choose his own way in life, but – if only he hadn't walked right out of our lives, the way he did. We might have grandchildren, and we don't even know it.'

She was gazing into the fireplace, her face wistful. Fleetingly, Matt saw sorrow beneath the toughness. Gwynnie was the one who'd been in hospital, but Matt realised that she looked after Wil as much as he looked after her. More, perhaps.

'I don't know why I came out with all that,' she said. 'Maundering on! You must be bored silly.'

'No, it's OK.'

Gwynnie looked at him, putting on a brighter face. 'Still, we look after each other, Wil and me. We've got each other, and we've got Jacko. Wil wouldn't have coped without Jacko, this last couple of weeks. His pride and joy, that dog is. Aren't you, boy?' she added, as Jacko came into the room, his claws clicking on the stone floor. Behind him came Wil, picking his way carefully with the tea tray.

'I got you Coke,' he told Matt. 'Remembered after last time, you don't much go for tea. Coke, you always liked.'

'Wil,' said Gwynnie. 'This is Matt. Not Owen.'

Wil looked puzzled, before saying, 'Yes. Yes, I know that.'

'But I do like Coke,' Matt added quickly, glad not to be faced with Wil's strong syrupy tea.

Jacko was waiting attentively. Wil said

something that sounded like *'Gorr-weth lowr,'* and at once he lay down on the hearth rug, still watching Wil's face.

'That's Welsh, isn't it?' Matt asked.

'It is,' said Wil. *'Gorwedd lawr* – lie down. He understands every word. Understands a lot more than some people, if you ask me.' He lowered the tray to the table, his hands shaking with the effort of holding it steady.

'I saw you herding sheep with him,' Matt said awkwardly. 'The other night. It looked good.'

'Oh, aye. We still do a bit, for Lewis up the way there. Jacko enjoys it. He's a working dog – he doesn't like sitting about.'

'I'd really like to be able to train a dog like that,' said Matt. 'It'd be great!'

'You would?' Wil looked at him closely. 'Well, Jacko likes you. That's a start. There's some people got a way with dogs, and some haven't.'

Matt thought of Wil and Jacko out in the field, working together, so closely that you'd think they had one brain between them. Wil on his own was a frail old man with shaking hands; Wil with Jacko was two sharp, alert minds and a quick set of responses.

'Wil, why don't you take Jacko out to the orchard, when we've had tea?' Gwynnie said. 'Show Matt what he can do.'

Wil swallowed tea with a slurp and a gulp. 'If you want.'

Matt's mind snagged on the thought of Tig and Robbo waiting outside, watching. 'I'd like that,' he said. 'I mean, I'd really, really like it a lot. But I've got to go.' He swigged down the Coke faster than felt comfortable; it fizzed gassily inside him. 'Thanks for the drink. And I'm sorry about – you know.'

'You're not a bad boy,' Gwynnie said. 'I can tell. But if you want my advice – and why should you, but I'll give it you anyway – you'll be careful who you go around with. Come back another day.'

Wil spoke to her rapidly in Welsh. Gwynnie listened intently, then gave him a quick reply.

'Well, er – bye, then.' Matt went to the door and closed it behind him, knowing he'd have Tig and Robbo to face.

He couldn't think quickly enough. What was he going to *tell* them? That he'd sat down and had a nice chat and a glass of Coke? And that Martin was nothing to do with it? But no, Martin *was*. He was always waiting in the background. And now Owen, the other lost boy. Where was *he*, and was that Wil's fault as well?

Talking to each other in Welsh, so that he couldn't understand – that was a bit unfair, wasn't it?

'Oi, Lank!' Tig loomed from behind the brambles. 'You took long enough. Did you put the frighteners on him?'

'Is he a gibbering wreck?' asked Robbo.

'No – look.' He'd have to put a stop to this. 'It won't work. He never thought I was Martin in the first place. He thought I was someone else.'

'See, I told you,' Rob said. 'He's screwy. Demented.'

'Yeah, well.' Matt squared up to him. 'If you're right, that makes it a bit unfair, doesn't it? Picking on him, making him confused?'

'Fair?' Tig said angrily. 'Fair? What's *fair* got to do with it? Was it fair what he did to that kid down there, and what he did to—You're useless, Lank, as much use as a wet rag. Should have known. Soon as you get in there, you're all *Yes, Wil. No, Wil. Three bags full, Wil.* You'd believe anything he told you.'

'He didn't tell me anything,' Matt retorted. 'Anyway, Gwynnie's home now. She's there. It was never going to work.'

'Oh, *Gwynnie*,' Tig mocked. 'You're well in, then. What did you do – sit down and have a nice cup of tea?'

Matt's face flushed hotly. He couldn't be sure they hadn't looked through the window – except that, surely, Jacko would have barked.

'Stuff it,' he told Tig. 'I've had it with this. I'm going.' He mounted his bike and pushed off into the lane.

'Yeah, right,' Tig called after him. 'You clear off home back to Mummy and Daddy. I'll sort this out myself.'

FIFTEEN

Adam

Something was going to happen to Wil. Matt knew it. Something bad. And it would be his fault; he'd screwed up, bottled out.

Why hadn't he lied to Tig? Said that yes, he'd pretended to be Martin, and Wil had gone mental, started raving or foaming at the mouth, or whatever Tig wanted to hear? Only problem, he wasn't a good liar; not good enough to fool Tig.

What was he going to *do*? He couldn't simply go home and forget about it. And it was no use telling himself it wasn't his problem. It was. He hadn't wanted to get involved, but had let himself get pulled in.

If he went home and told Mum and Dad what had happened . . . but that would mean getting himself into trouble, for sure. Mum already had doubts about Tig; she'd go ballistic if she knew about the baiting of Wil.

Tell *Adam*. That made more sense. Adam knew

more than Mum and Dad did, about the people involved.

How, though? He imagined himself saying to Adam, 'I keep seeing Martin. He wants me to do something, I don't know what.' No, impossible. Adam would think he was making it up, or playing a joke.

Still, he couldn't do *nothing.*

Before he could have second thoughts, he stopped at the public phone box by the craft centre, got the farm number from enquiries, and dialled.

Thankfully, it wasn't Bryn or Sian who picked up, but their mother. Without saying who it was, Matt asked for Adam, and a few moments later he came to the phone.

'Hello, Adam here?'

'Adam, it's Matt.'

'Hi! You OK?'

'No,' Matt said quickly. 'Look, I've got to ask you some things. And tell you some things. It's about Tig. And Wil Jones. And Martin Lloyd.'

'What, then?'

'I can't tell you on the phone,' Matt said, one eye on the street outside. 'It's too complicated.'

There was a moment's pause, then: 'I'll be in Hay this afternoon with Bryn, to get a birthday present for Sian. D'you want to meet us? Say, at the Granary? Half-three?'

Matt agreed, and went on home, feeling a little better. When Mum and Dad asked where he'd been, he fended them off with 'Just out on my bike,' but felt bad because he could lie to them more successfully than he could to Tig. Not that it *was* a lie, exactly, but it wasn't a truthful answer, either. It occurred to him that, with Gwynnie knowing exactly who he was, it wouldn't be long before she came into the shop with Wil, and then his secret would be out.

Dad was talking about arranging some kind of family outing over Easter. 'We can easily do it. Get the guests' breakfast and clear up, and go off somewhere, the four of us. Fen's got some time off, hasn't she? It'll do her good to drag herself away from her books.'

'There's something wrong with her.' The words were out of Matt's mouth before he'd decided to say them.

Mum looked at him. 'Wrong with Fen? What d'you mean, Matty?'

'She's not working any more. In her room, I mean. She just lies there and stares at the ceiling.'

Dad looked bemused. 'Is that bad?'

'It is with Fen,' Matt mumbled. 'You know what she's like with schoolwork. She says she can't do it any more.'

'Can't do it?'

'She sits and stares at her books and they don't make sense.'

'No!' Mum put down a half-eaten sandwich. 'She's never said! This is our fault,' she said to Dad. 'I knew it'd make things hard for her, moving at the start of the Sixth Form. And she's so good at keeping things to herself!'

'She's a big worrier,' Dad agreed. 'Pushes herself too hard. Much too hard.'

'Right.' Matt hovered, on the brink of breaking his promise; Mum and Dad both looked at him, and he plunged on: 'Last couple of weeks, she's been working in the middle of the night. Writing essays at three in the morning. In her sleep, even.'

Mum looked stricken. 'And I never knew! No *wonder* she's been looking tired. Doing all that *and* her café job – and now she's stopped working, you say, and she's fretting about that?'

Matt nodded, uneasy.

'Who can stop her, though?' said Dad. 'You know what she's like – how obstinate. The more we tell her to go easier on herself, the more determined she'll be.'

'But it sounds like she's reached burnout.' Absentmindedly, Mum began stacking the plates. 'And it's the *holidays*. She needs to give herself some time off.'

'We've got to get her out of that room,' said Dad.

'Have a meal out, or go and see a film. Have some days out, like I was saying. I'm glad you told us, Matt.'

'Yeah, well. You know.' Matt examined a scuff on one of his trainers. Had he really done something right, for once? But the promise. Now Fen could break hers, too. Would that matter, now that he didn't want Tig as his friend? If *friend* was what Tig had ever been.

'I'll have a talk with her. As soon as she gets in,' said Mum, getting up to run water at the sink. 'I'm off now to see a man about some books. Are you busy, Matt, or d'you want to help Dad in the shop?'

'I'm going out again. Meeting Bryn in town. He's getting a birthday present for Sian.'

'Oh – is the twins' birthday coming up?' Mum said. 'Do you want to get them something?'

Durr! It hadn't dawned on Matt that if it was Sian's birthday, it was Bryn's as well.

'Dunno,' he said. 'What'd I get, for both of them?'

'I don't mind helping you choose,' Mum offered. 'I love buying presents. You can invite the twins over, some time, if you like – you've been there a few times now.'

Eager to meet Bryn and Adam, Matt got to the Granary first, and stood outside by the Market Cross. He soon saw them, coming down Broad

Street, laughing at something. Bryn was alive with excitement. He called out, as soon as Matt was within hailing distance, 'Guess what we're getting for our birthday?'

'What?'

'A puppy!' Bryn jogged up to him, followed more slowly by Adam. 'A border collie! From a family of working dogs. We're going to train him ourselves. We can't have him yet, but we've been over and chosen the one we want, and we can have him in a month's time when he's old enough to leave his mother.'

Matt was envious. 'Are there others, then? A litter?'

'Yes, four, only two of the others have already got homes.'

'So there's still one left?'

'Matt,' said Adam. 'You can't keep a collie in a town house, if that's what you're thinking. It wouldn't be happy. They need space, and work.'

'I know,' Matt said reluctantly. 'Mum and Dad would never let me, and anyway we've got cats. There's cat people and dog people, Mum says, and they're cat people.'

But he couldn't help dreaming about it while they joined the queue inside: him and a puppy, roaming the hills and fields! He'd train it perfectly, as well as Wil had trained Jacko, and it would be his very own dog. He'd be good at it, he knew he would.

'You can help with ours if you want,' said Bryn. 'Like, can you think of a good name? He hasn't got one yet.'

Matt could only think of Jacko.

Some of the tables were taken, but the café wasn't as crowded as at lunchtime. They found a corner table and unloaded their tray; Adam looked at Matt.

'OK, then,' he prompted. 'What's all this about?'

What *was* it all about – where was the best place to start? Matt launched in: 'Well, you know that book? The one you lent me?'

Adam nodded. 'The Tommy Jones story?'

'Yeah. Well, I saw the name *Martin Lloyd* written in the front, and I knew about Martin being killed on his bike, cos I'd seen the cross on the lane, on that dead tree. His initials are the same as mine.'

'M.L. – oh yes,' said Adam. 'That must have been creepy.'

'Bryn told me Martin was your friend.'

'Yes, he was. When he – when he died, after the funeral and everything, his mum invited me round to their house, to choose something of his to keep. Martin and I did the Pen-y-Fan and obelisk walk together only a couple of weeks before, with his dad, and his dad bought him the Tommy Jones book at the visitors' centre, after, so that's what I chose. That and a couple of drawings from Mart's sketchbook. He was brilliant at drawing. Cartoony things.'

I already knew that, Matt thought, with the strange prickly sensation he had when Martin was around.

'Right,' he said. It was hard to keep a grip on things, to tell them in an order that made sense. 'Then Wil Jones keeps coming into our shop, with books to sell, and someone – well, someone told me it was him that killed Martin, in his van. Hit and run – drove off and left him to – to die in the road—'

Adam looked at him. 'Yes, and it'll take me about two seconds to guess who it was that told you.'

'Tig,' said Bryn.

'What?' Matt's eyes went from one face to the other.

'It wasn't Wil's fault,' said Adam. 'It was Martin's.'

'But—'

'It was an accident. Martin was riding fast downhill on his bike, down the steep hill from Gospel Pass. He didn't slow down in time for the turn. Wil was driving along and didn't have time to swerve – Martin crashed straight into him. Wasn't wearing a helmet, either.' Adam looked down at the coffee mug in front of him as if surprised to find it there; he held it in both hands, but still didn't drink.

They were all silent for a few moments.

That's exactly what happened to me, Matt thought. *There, in the same place. What I thought happened.*

'It's funny,' he said, 'the tree being dead, too. Like it's died in sympathy.' It sounded daft, but now he'd said it.

Adam looked up at him. 'I don't suppose it is. It's an oak, isn't it? They're the last trees to come into leaf, oak and ash.'

Matt nodded, not knowing much about trees, and more concerned with taking in this new account of the accident. 'How can you *know* what happened? Anyway, Wil admits it's his fault – he told me!'

'What, you didn't go and *ask* him?' said Bryn.

'I think, if it were me – if I'd been involved in an accident that killed someone – I'd think it was my fault. Wouldn't you?' Adam said to Matt. 'What must it be like – forever thinking *if only* this and *if only* that? If only Wil hadn't come along along just then – if only he'd stayed a bit longer at the pub – if only Martin had braked sooner, or gone a different way—' He looked down at his hands, clasped round the mug. 'Me, too. I was supposed to have gone with him that day, with Martin, over to

Capel-y-ffin on our bikes – only I didn't, because my aunt and uncle turned up and I preferred to kick a football about with my cousins. So there's another *if only* – if only they hadn't dropped by, if only I'd already left – if I'd been with Martin I could have shouted out, yelled at him to slow down.'

'You can't say it was *your* fault,' Matt objected. 'You might as well say "if only Martin had never been born" or "if only bikes had never been invented."'

'Well, anyway. Wil thinks it was his fault,' Adam said, 'and that's why he doesn't come down to town much. In a little place like this, where people know each other, they remember things. I suppose he thinks everyone's blaming him.'

'He might even bump into Martin's parents,' said Matt. 'How awful would that be?'

'No, they moved away soon after. Moved up to Rhayader,' Adam told him. 'But I bet that's why Wil chose your mum's shop, Matt, when he wanted to sell books.'

'Of all the bookshops to choose from in Hay,' Bryn said, understanding, 'he picked the one where nobody knows him, or Martin.'

'So,' Adam went on, 'to answer your question. There was a witness – a woman riding her horse along the lane. She saw exactly what happened –

saw that Wil had no chance, Martin went smack into him. It wasn't hit and run, either. She tried to look after Martin, while Wil drove off to call the police and ambulance. People didn't carry mobile phones all the time, back then. There was an inquest, police, all that sort of thing. But Wil was never blamed for what happened.'

Matt gazed at the chair-back of the next table, at someone's red padded coat; a snatch of conversation sounded loud in his ears: 'No, you want to try *steaming* them, then eat them with melted butter.' His thoughts swept him back to the rush downhill, the irresistible whizz and swoosh of it, the careless giving-over of himself to speed and pleasure; then the Land Rover, the face at the wheel, the juddering impact. The café, the customers and waitresses blurred into background. Then he realised that both Adam and Bryn were looking at him, waiting for him to say something.

'So – so why's Tig got such a thing about it?' he managed.

'Because he's Tig,' said Bryn.

'Because of his brother,' said Adam.

'His brother?'

'Luke, the guy we saw the other night. He used to be a friend of mine too, mine and Martin's. Till he started getting into bad stuff. Nicking sweets or fags from shops at first. Then he got bigger ideas – car radios, leather coats, whatever he could find. There's plenty about, in cars, with all the tourists here. He ended up doing a couple of months in a young offenders' place, and Wil helped put him there.'

'Wil did?' Matt echoed.

Adam nodded. 'Luke took money from a garage on the Brecon road, got it from the till, and Wil saw. He had his dog with him—'

'Jacko?'

'That's right. Jacko got Luke cornered and Wil yelled for help – the owner was in the storeroom. The owner called the police, and that was Luke nicked. He'd been cautioned before, so this time he was put inside. Now he's out, got no job, and hanging round with not much to do.'

Matt sat in silence, taking all this in.

'As for Tig,' Adam continued, 'it's not fair to judge him by his brother, but he'll go the same way if he's not careful.'

Matt didn't want to start explaining how closely he'd been involved, but Bryn knew he went around with Tig and Rob – *had* been going around with them – and understood. 'He knew he could string you along,' Bryn said. 'You're new. You want to watch out – you know, at school. He's trouble, only clever as well. You don't have to stick with him and Robbo. There's always Sian and me, and James.'

Matt nodded. School seemed a long way off;

159

there was more urgent business to worry about. 'Tig's going to do something up at Wil's,' he said unhappily. 'Something bad.'

'What d'you think he might do?' Adam looked at him closely; Matt shook his head.

'Have you warned him?' Bryn said. 'Wil, I mean? Your mum knows Wil, doesn't she – couldn't she ring him?'

'I'd phone the police, if I were Wil,' said Adam. 'It's a lonely spot up there.'

'Right.' Matt felt relieved. Wil wasn't a callous killer after all, and airing his problems to Adam and Bryn made them feel less weighty.

'Hey,' Bryn said. 'You know the dog we're getting? He's coming from a farm at Boughrood, the same place as Wil's Jacko. Same bitch, same line of working dogs. Our Ifor, as well – they're all related. So he's Jacko's half-brother, maybe even full brother!'

'Yeah? He'll be brilliant, then.'

Bryn nodded, and swigged down the last of his drink. 'Are we going to get this present, then? And what about the Nedd Gorge – can we fix a day for that?'

'Monday, if you like,' Adam said. 'Want to come, Matt?'

'You bet. Where is it?'

Adam began moving the salt and pepper pots on

the table. 'We're here, right, in Hay. That's Brecon; this is Merthyr; the Nedd Gorge runs from here down to about there. What we'll do is park the car *here*—'

Matt had vaguely noticed Fen earlier, clearing tables, and now she came over to theirs. She picked up Matt's and Bryn's empty glasses and reached for Adam's mug before noticing it was still half-full; at the same moment Adam extended a hand to stop her from taking it. Their fingers touched; both flinched back. 'Sorry!' said Adam, and 'Sorry!' said Fen in the same instant. Then – not having registered that it was Matt sitting there – she noticed him. 'Oh! Matt.'

'She's my sister,' Matt said, to explain to Adam; Bryn knew, from school. 'Fen.'

'Hi!' said Adam. 'I've seen you here before.'

'Have you?' Fen was going pink. 'It's nice of you to take Matt on all those hikes and things. Keeps him out of trouble.'

'No problem,' said Adam. 'We're planning another day, as it happens. Monday – waterfalls in the Nedd Gorge. Come with us, if you like the sound of it. The café'll be closed, won't it?'

Fen, take a day off to go walking around waterfalls! Matt waited for her to say, 'I can't, I've got too much to do.' But instead, she balanced the tray carefully with both hands and said, 'Thanks! I

161

might do that.' Then she turned to the next table and started clattering cups and plates.

Adam looked pleased; Bryn caught Matt's eye and gave a small smirk. What was going on? Matt wasn't sure he wanted Fen tagging along, and she'd never shown much interest in walking before. Didn't even have a decent pair of boots, as far as he knew. She'd probably get a blister, or twist her ankle, and start whingeing; he hoped Adam knew what he was letting himself in for.

They parted outside the café. Bryn and Adam headed back to the jewellery shop in the craft centre, for Sian's present; Matt towards home. On an impulse, he diverted to the phone box at the corner of Bear Street, searched his memory for Wil's number, and dialled. While the ringtone sounded he tried to think of something plausible to say. After a long while Wil answered, sounding puffed. Maybe he'd hurried in from the orchard.

'It's Matt. I phoned to—' *Quick, think of something!* To see if you're OK, would have been the truth. '—to say, er—' *Inspiration!* 'You know you said, I mean Gwynnie said – I mean, er, Mrs Jones said – you could show me some of the things Jacko does, I mean teach me a bit?'

'Matt, you say?' Wil was obviously struggling to keep up. 'Matt, from the bookshop? You came here, when was it – oh, today?'

'Yes. Matt Lanchester. It was this morning. Could you, some time, could you show me what Jacko does?'

'Right you are, boy,' Wil said, cottoning on. 'You come tomorrow, early but not too early, and we'll give the old dog a workout.'

'Thanks! That'll be great.'

Matt rang off, vastly relieved. Wil didn't sound in the least perturbed; Tig and Rob wouldn't have hung around up there all this time. So nothing had gone wrong, and tomorrow was another day.

SIXTEEN

Mist

There was that old saying, Matt thought, about a problem shared being a problem halved. Maybe it was true, but you could also say that every problem solved threw up a new one. OK, he definitely wasn't going to link himself with Tig and Rob any more, in school or out, but that meant Tig would make things unpleasant in ways only he could think of.

But now there was today. Good Friday, and he was going up to Wil's – openly, this time, and for a nice reason. Anticipation sharpened his movements as he got up and dressed. The weather didn't look good – grey and blowy – but he'd go anyway. He didn't want to miss this; he wanted to see Jacko work, wanted to learn some useful things for helping Bryn and Sian with their puppy, when they got it. He'd prove that he had a way with dogs, like Wil said.

Fen wasn't working today, as the café was closed.

It seemed daft, Matt thought, to close at Easter, when surely there'd be more tourists around, but that was how it was. As he went downstairs for breakfast he heard her in her room, talking excitedly on her mobile: 'Yes, Monday. No, it's not exactly – but who knows – anyway, I can't work *all* the time. I'll get it done – I always do—' A few minutes later, coming down to the kitchen, she said that she was spending today with her friend Anna. Matt looked at her suspiciously. He'd never work out what went on in girls' heads – especially Fen's.

Loud bangs sounded from the cellar; Dad was putting up shelves. There were two lots of guests staying, and Mum was whizzing in and out of the dining-room, shooing cats from under her feet as she carried in teapots and toast racks and enormous platefuls of fried breakfast. When the phone rang, she called out, 'Get that, someone, can you?'

Fen went; Matt took another slice of toast. 'It was for you,' Fen said, coming back. 'Someone called Gwynnie. She says Jacko's gone missing. Who's Gwynnie? Who's Jacko?'

Jacko.

Jacko would never wander off, or get lost, unless—

—unless someone had taken him, stolen him—

Tig. It must be!

A horrible sense of foreboding shuddered through Matt's body. It was the sort of thing Tig would think of. Doing something to Jacko was the best way of getting at Will.

'Is that all she said?' Matt demanded.

'Something about no point going up there. Going up where?'

There was no time to explain. 'I've got to go. Tell Mum, will you?'

'*You* tell her—'

But Matt was already on his way, pulling on his sweatshirt. He stopped in the hallway to grab the phone and dial the twins' number. Thank goodness, he could hear Mum's voice in the dining-room – she'd stopped to chat to the guests – and it was Adam who picked up the phone.

'Adam? Gwynnie just rang – she said Jacko's disappeared.'

'Disappeared?'

'Gone. I bet Tig's taken him!'

'But a trained dog like Jacko'd never go off with anyone,' said Adam. 'Not willingly. He'd have to be dragged, or drugged, or—'

Or worse than that.

'I'm going up there,' Matt said.

'I'll come over as well. Have they called the police?'

'Don't know. I'll find out when I get there.'

He was on his bike and cycling fast before he remembered: Tig was afraid of dogs. Afraid of Jacko, anyway. Matt thought of the look in Tig's eyes when Jacko had herded him and Robbo up the lane; Tig hadn't liked being teased about it, either, his weak spot. If anyone had lured Jacko away, it must have been Rob, who would do whatever Tig told him. Tig, as well as his brother, had grudges against both Wil *and* his dog. This was the perfect revenge.

But how? Where, and for how long? And had Wil realised?

It was an awful day for cycling, for dog-walking or for anything else outside. By the time he was clear of the town and pedalling hard uphill, the fields and copses were all cloaked in haze, and clouds louring darkly over the Black Mountains; the air was damp with the first spatterings of rain. Good job he'd grabbed his coat on the way out of the house. He rode as fast as he could, and almost missed the forked track to Dan-y-fforest.

Dumping his bike by the gate, he hurried up the front path. It was Gwynnie who answered his loud knock at the door: she came slowly, leaning on her stick, and scanned his face.

'Oh, it's you – Matt. You shouldn't have come

up, not in this weather! There's Wil out in it already, likely to catch his death! I've called Lewis from the farm – he's gone after him in the Discovery.'

'Wil's gone out?'

'Yes, up the lane there, said he was going to look for Jacko in the fields, and up on the common. He won't rest till he finds that dog!'

'Did he phone the police?'

'No – I wanted to, but Wil wouldn't have it. Said he'd have a good look himself, first. Only now the rain's coming on.'

'I'm going too,' Matt told her.

Gwynnie looked doubtful. 'Well, I don't know – wouldn't it be better to—'

'No! I'm going – I've got to!'

'Only as far as the cattle grid, then. I don't want you getting lost as well. Wait!' Gwynnie called, as Matt ran down the path. 'Take his coat – and don't you be long, now.'

Matt went back for it; it was a bulky thing, heavy and waxed. He put it round his own shoulders like a cloak, the easiest way to carry it on his bike. He had no intention of cycling tamely up to the cattle grid and back, like Gwynnie said – he was heading for the high fields behind the farm, and the bike wasn't going to be much use up there.

A few moments later he was in the yard of Ardwyn Farm, wondering which way Wil had gone. The yard was bordered by a house on one side and outbuildings on the other three, with various bits of farm machinery in a corner. There was no one about, only a group of calves surveying him from an open-sided barn, their breath making clouds as they snorted and backed away. Everything looked forlorn and rain-soaked.

Abandoning the bike, he found a gap between barns, where a rutted track led through a gateway and up to rough pasture. This way? Pausing, Matt thought he heard – half lost in the wind and the rain – the sound of a whistle, like the one Wil used with Jacko. He strained his ears – there it was again, weak, but carried towards him, from higher ground ahead. He set off in pursuit.

'Wil!' he yelled. 'Wil!'

Wil must be searching where he'd searched before, for Owen. Always, always, Jacko was his companion, but now Wil was searching alone.

Matt waded on through thick grass. He wasn't as fit as he thought he was; the steepness soon told on his legs and his lungs, and he was sweating inside his jacket, encumbered by Wil's heavy coat; as it slipped sideways off his shoulders he bundled it up and carried it instead. As soon as he moved on, the swish of wet grass and his own breathing obscured the thin note of the whistle, so that he began to think he'd imagined it. Stopping again to listen, he thought he heard it again – ahead, higher up, some way off. Or was it only the call of a bird?

'Wil!' he shouted again. 'Wil!'

The word was snatched by the wind and carried down the valley, not up towards the common. The mist closed in, damp and clammy, blurring everything into paleness. He'd never find Wil; the whistle was his only hope. If only *he* had one, to signal back!

Something was moving along the hedge ahead of him; the grey shape of a dog. It stopped on a rise of ground, stood, and looked round at him, waiting for him to catch up.

'Jacko?' he shouted.

No, it couldn't be! It was bigger than Jacko, and sleeker; grey, not black-and-white, though he couldn't see well enough to be sure. As he plunged towards it, it moved on along the hedge, lifting its legs high above the tussocky grass. Again, it stopped and waited, looking at him. This time Matt heard the whistle loud and clear: closer. Higher and higher he plodded, occasionally breaking into a run, then tiring and slowing to rest. Each time he thought he'd reached a ridge, the land stretched on beyond. When he turned and looked back, he could no longer see the farm; he saw no buildings at all, only hedges, and stunted trees, bent and leaning, battered by years of wind.

This is what happened to Tommy Jones, he thought, anxiety edging into fear. *This is how it was with him, going higher than he meant, getting lost in the hills.* The idea slipped into his mind that if he got tired he could lie down and sleep, and the dog would wait until he woke up. *Don't be daft – no way!* He wasn't five years old, and he wasn't tired, even if – he paused to look round again – he was more or less lost. But how lost could he possibly be? Up was towards the Black Mountains and Gospel Pass; down was towards the farm, and Dan-y-fforest. If he kept his head, he'd be OK. Find Wil first, though. He couldn't go down without Wil.

The dog leaped over a high hedge and disappeared from view. There was no gate or stile, and Matt had no choice but to scramble half-through, half-over, getting snagged on thorns and scratched by brambles. On the other side was only open moorland and the rise towards the pass. The dog was nowhere in sight, but far ahead of him – over another rise in the ground – he heard barking, and the faintest of whistles.

'Wait, can't you!' he shouted. He had the feeling

that he could stumble on for ever, out of the real world in this pearly-pale dreamscape where everything looked the same, where he had no map and compass to show him the way, where there was nothing to see but sedgy grass, and sheep and ponies taking what shelter they could find against the hedge. Nothing but mist and cloud and loneliness.

But the dog was excited now; it had seen something, over the ridge. It ran in a tight circle; it barked and barked; it ran a few steps towards Matt, then immediately back to the same place.

Dreading what he might see, Matt hurried after it. There was something – someone – hunched on the ground.

Matt blinked moisture away from his eyelashes. The rain was coming down harder now; he hadn't noticed how much, in the effort of pursuit. He came closer, skirting round so as not to approach from behind. Wil – yes, it was Wil – was sitting on the ground, on the wet grass, quite still, with his legs and feet in a small hollow.

'Wil?' Matt called.

Slowly, Wil raised his head and looked at him. He gave no response.

'You can't stop here! It's cold and wet and—' Matt looked around desperately. There was no one in sight, no building, no road – and the dog, too, seemed to have slunk away when he wasn't looking.

He tried again. 'Come on! We're going home. I'll help find Jacko. Please!' He tugged at Wil's arm, at the sleeve of his sweater, and felt how wet it was, how rain-sogged. 'Here! Put this on.' Unbundling the coat, he showed it to Wil and tried to help him on with it. Wil understood, and put his arms through the sleeves, but was slow and numbed with cold. He had on his tweed cap, and his waistcoat, but it wasn't enough. You could *die* in weather like this, if you didn't have enough warm clothes or enough food – Matt knew that from Adam. You didn't have to be caught in a snowstorm to die of exposure. Between them, they'd done everything wrong – no map, no compass, nothing to eat or drink, inadequate clothes. They had to keep *moving*.

He tried another tactic. 'Come on, Wil! I'm not going back without you. I'm tired and wet and hungry, even if you're not.'

Wil began to speak, with an effort. 'I know who you are, now.' He peered at Matt; his voice was so thin and croaky that Matt had to bend close to hear him at all. 'I get confused – I've got myself in a muddle, haven't I? Even thought you were my boy, my Owen. But it's you, isn't it? You won't

173

leave me alone, will you – won't let me forget! You needn't worry. I never will forget. Never, as long as I live.'

'What? Forget what?'

'You know! That night. On the lane. A night like any other. One minute was all it took, one minute. I've gone over and over and over it in my mind, wishing it was different. One minute, and nothing's ever the same again. Only you didn't give me a chance, did you? If only I'd seen you in time, swerved—'

He thinks I'm Martin.

'I killed you.' Wil bent forward, shaking his head. 'I killed you, and nothing can change that.'

Tell him. Tell him. The voice was pounding in his ears like headache, like earache: insistent, throbbing, excited. And Matt realised: *this* was what Martin wanted. This was what it was all for. Not for punishment, not for revenge. Martin wanted Wil to *know*.

Matt took a deep breath. 'Wil,' he said loudly. 'It wasn't your fault. It was his. Martin's. I'm not Martin, but I know what happened. I was there. I – I saw.' Should he have said that? But it was too late now – he had, and Wil showed no surprise. He merely sat blinking and listening, gazing into the mist.

'You didn't have a chance,' Matt went on. 'Martin

was – he was carried away with the speed, the fun of it. He came whizzing down that hill and right into your path. You didn't have time to do anything. You tried to swerve – you were desperate – you'd have done anything rather than hit him. But he slammed right into you.'

Wil listened in silence.

'You mustn't blame yourself,' Matt said. 'You mustn't. Everyone knows it wasn't your fault. You can't keep going over and over it.'

Wil's head drooped lower; he made a whimpering sound. Matt realised he was crying: he began to sob, big choking sobs that heaved his shoulders. After a few moments he rummaged in his jacket pocket and pulled out a huge handkerchief, blew his nose loudly and sniffed a few times. Matt was dismayed; he'd never seen a grown man cry before, not like that. What now?

Likely to catch his death, Gwynnie had said. That was a saying, but people often spoke the truth without knowing – what if his death *was* what Wil had caught?

'Wil, we're going home now,' Matt said briskly. 'Time to go.'

Wil baulked. 'I'm staying here.'

'But Gwynnie's worried sick! Is that what you want?'

'I'm no use to her,' said Wil. 'No use to anyone.'

'That's rubbish!' Matt tugged at his arm. 'What would Gwynnie do without you? And we've got to find Jacko!'

'He's gone,' Wil said, mournful and hopeless. 'Gone.'

'Come on! We won't find him without you!'

Wil gave a heavy sigh, but seemed to give in. He began to lurch stiffly to his feet; leaning against Matt for support, he stumbled, almost tripped. But this was better; there was some chance, now, of walking slowly back down, finding the cattle grid gates and the road down towards the farm.

Which way? Matt peered through the mist, and thought he saw the dog – below them now, waiting.

'Where's your whistle? Your dog whistle?' he asked Wil.

'I had it. My hands got numb and I dropped it,' Wil said, through lips purplish-blue with cold.

Never mind. This dog didn't need whistling. He turned and trotted off, out of sight again below a ridge. Following with painful slowness, hampered by Wil's stumpy gait, Matt saw that he was leading them to a track – a narrow sheep track, hardly more than an indentation in the ground – that plunged down the hillside.

'He showed me where you were,' Matt said to Wil; 'the dog there. He knows the way. If we follow him we'll be all right.'

Wil peered into the mist. 'Dog? I can't see any dog.'

'There!' said Matt, pointing.

But now he couldn't see the grey shape, either.

Jacko

'Wil! Matt!'

The darker shapes ahead gradually came into focus. Hedge. Gate. Cattle grid barring the road. Almost dizzy with relief, Matt was guiding Wil down the slope towards them when, unmistakably, their names were called, followed by the piercing note of a whistle. Wil stopped, cocking his head like a dog; then he whistled back. Even with no plastic whistle, he could do what Matt could never achieve no matter how hard he tried – produce a loud, shrill note simply by hissing through his teeth.

They both stood in the rain, waiting.

Matt heard him before he saw him – his panting breath, the soft squelching rhythm of paws galloping on mud – then Jacko hurtled towards them, in great joyous bounds, and leaped up at Wil, licking his face and almost knocking him backwards. Wil gathered the wriggling dog in both arms and held him firm, speaking in Welsh.

'Jacko! Where—' Matt strained his eyes through the haze. Three figures were coming towards them – a tall person, flanked by two smaller ones.

Adam, Bryn and Sian.

Everyone started talking at once. 'How did you—'

'Where—'

'I don't believe it—'

'Thank God you've found him—'

'I thought—'

'All that can wait,' said Adam, taking charge. 'Let's get Wil home. He's soaked through – so's Matt.'

Adam's car was by the cattle grid. The three children piled into the back, while Wil got into the passenger seat with Jacko pressed against his legs. Matt saw that Jacko hardly took his eyes off Wil's face; in fact, he could have sworn that the dog was smiling.

Having been tearful again when Jacko first appeared, Wil was now bewildered, and a little embarrassed at all the fuss. 'I don't know why you're going to so much bother,' he protested, while Adam helped him fasten his seat belt. 'I can walk back, no problem.'

'It's no trouble,' Adam said, reversing.

Matt wondered if Wil knew who Adam was; but

Wil submitted now to being driven, and asked no questions. The car interior steamed up gently from everyone's damp clothes. As the tyres clanked over the grid, Matt rubbed at the side window and looked back, wondering where the other dog had gone, the grey dog that had led him to Wil. Not a sign. By now, Matt was wondering if he'd only imagined him – made himself a dog out of a swirl of mist.

Down at the cottage, Gwynnie was waiting with the door ajar; she ushered them all in, surprised to see so many people. The fire was lit, the lamps on, and the cottage a sanctuary of warmth after the rawness of the hillside. Gwynnie phoned Lewis's mobile to tell him Wil was safe; then she took Wil straight upstairs to change into dry clothes, and brought Matt a knitted sweater to put on. 'Owen's,' she told him. 'A bit big, but it'll do.'

Jacko stretched himself in front of the fire, Gwynnie went through to the kitchen to make hot drinks for everyone, and at last Adam could explain what had been going on.

'When you phoned, I got the twins together and we set off for here,' he told Matt, 'only then I had a better idea. We went straight to the Jenkinses' house—'

'The minute we got there we heard Jacko barking,' said Sian, who was sprawled on the hearth rug, one arm round Jacko's neck. 'He was locked in their shed!'

Bryn joined in. 'No sign of Luke, *or* Tig—'

'Only a neighbour, at first—'

'She'd had enough of Jacko's barking—'

'Came out soon as she saw us, cos she thought it was Luke come back,' said Sian. '*Hope someone shuts up that dog,* she went—'

'That *effing* dog, is what she said,' Bryn corrected.

'*—that effing dog, it's doing my head in, barking non-stop.* And then Tig's mum came out—'

'And you could tell she'd had enough of it, too. *Have you come for that dog?* she goes, and Ad says yes, only what *she* meant was had we come to *buy* him—'

'Hang on,' interrupted Matt. 'They'd stuck him in their shed, and they were going to *sell* him?'

'Jacko's a trained working dog – intelligent, keen – he'd be worth a thousand or more,' Adam told him. 'Only he'd have to be sold with no questions asked, or answered.'

'So why didn't you call the police?' Matt asked.

Sian and Bryn both looked at Adam.

'Mm. That's what I was going to do, at first,' he said. 'But then I took a gamble. I hope it's worked.'

'Gamble?'

'What Luke didn't reckon on, is Jacko's a one-man dog. Some dogs'll work for anyone – others, only for the person they know. Jacko's one of those. Besides, he's been trained to follow Welsh commands! He doesn't answer to English, and certainly not to Luke, but Luke didn't realize that. Once he'd got hold of Jacko, he couldn't do a thing with him, let alone show him off to a buyer—'

'And they're scared. Tig and Luke, both of them.' Bryn looked scathing.

'Scared of Jacko, who wouldn't hurt a fly!' Sian put her face close to the dog's. He licked her nose; she blinked and laughed.

'I should think he could be quite intimidating, if you tried to steal him,' Adam said.

'So how did they get him?' Matt asked. 'Did Tig's Mum tell you that?'

'No. Luke did,' said Adam.

'Luke?'

'She told me where to find him – round at the garage, where he works. So I went and had a chat.'

'While we waited in the car,' said Sian. 'We missed that bit.' She made a rueful face. 'I'm dying to know exactly what Ad said to Luke. He was in there ages.'

'It went more or less like this,' Adam said. 'I said to Luke, I know you've taken Wil's dog, and got him in your shed. He tried to deny it at first, then made up some story about finding him wandering in the street. Well, I knew that was a load of cobblers. He'd got a big sticking plaster on one hand, new and clean, so I asked what happened. He said he'd cut himself on an edge of metal. But I could tell he was lying, and eventually he said well OK then, he'd taken the dog from Wil's orchard early this morning, him and Tig. Got a lead on him – Luke said he was wearing thick gardening gloves but Jacko bit him all the same – and dragged him away. Just for a joke, he said, he'd meant to give him back later. Yeah, right, some joke, I told him. You can take him back if you want, he goes, I can't do a thing with him. What he *meant* was, he'd never be able to sell Jacko if he couldn't even get him out of the shed without getting bitten again.'

'But I still don't know why you wouldn't call the police?' Sian said.

Adam smiled. 'Thought I'd do a bit of bargaining.'

'Bargaining? With *Luke*?'

'It was really useful, that neighbour coming out and complaining,' said Adam. 'It means someone besides us knows Jacko was shut in the shed. *And* she heard Luke's mum ask if I'd come to buy him. It gave me a bit of leverage. What I said to Luke is: give me the dog, and I'll keep quiet. See, what I know, and Luke knows, is he's broken the terms of his release from the young offenders' place, by stealing Wil's dog. If the police hear about this, he'll be back inside.'

'And what's wrong with that?' Bryn demanded. 'Good job, if you ask me!'

Adam looked at him. 'There's Tig, isn't there? Tig's not likely to be put away. He'll be back at school with you lot, week after next.'

Matt looked into the glowing coals of the fire. He didn't want to think about that.

'Well, I don't see how you can stop Tig going to school,' Bryn stated. 'Not that he specially *wants* to – but he's stuck with it. And we're stuck with him.'

'No, that's right. So what I said to Luke is: you leave off bothering Wil, and so does Tig – you don't go near the place – or the police get to hear about what's happened. And Tig's not to stir up anything at school, or out of it, for any of you three – otherwise ditto.'

'And Luke agreed to that?' said Sian, sitting up.

'Didn't have much choice, did he?'

'And has Tig?'

'I had to leave that bit to Luke,' Adam said, 'to pass on.'

Matt thought about this. Adam had been clever, he decided: his bargaining meant that Luke got away with it, but it also avoided setting up any new grudges for either Luke or Tig. And now, with such good allies, Matt needn't worry about being intimidated.

Gwynnie brought in not only hot chocolate but the fruit cake called *bara brith*; a few moments later Wil came down, in fresh clothes, looking a bit puzzled at seeing so many people in the room, as if it were an unexpected party. Adam gave up the rocking-chair to Wil, and sat on the floor, and at once Jacko got up and moved close, sitting by Wil's legs.

'You haven't told us your bit, Matt,' Sian said.

Matt looked out of the window, towards the orchard; rain was still falling steadily. He couldn't begin to explain how strange it had felt up there on the hill, right out of the normal world.

'Nothing much to tell,' he answered. 'I went up the road and met Wil looking for Jacko – that's all.'

EIGHTEEN

Gwilym

Matt was cycling along Forest Road. On his own, the way he still liked to be, sometimes, even though he had real friends now.

The twins had come round for tea after school, and Matt had given them the birthday present he'd chosen with Mum – a smart collar and lead for their puppy. Not only that, but he'd given the puppy a name as well.

Gwilym.

Once it had occurred to him, Gwilym seemed the perfect name; Bryn and Sian, without knowing the reason, had liked it too.

'A good traditional name for a working dog,' Bryn said.

They'd given him a present too, though it wasn't his birthday. It was from Adam: a copy of a cartoony little picture Martin had drawn, one of the things Adam had chosen from Martin's belongings, to keep. The drawing showed Adam with the farm dog Ifor, standing by a gate in pouring rain, but because both Adam and the dog were eight years younger than they were now, it could easily have been Matt himself, with Jacko.

M.L., Martin had written in one corner.

Adam had scanned the picture into his computer and printed it out, and put it into an old photo frame for Matt. It was on Matt's bedside table, where he could look at it again later. It felt like seeing through Martin's eyes: seeing, drawing with quick lines, catching the likeness, enjoying his own skill.

Thanks, Martin.

Now Mrs Hughes had collected the twins, and Mum was getting ready for her drama group, and Fen had started going with Anna to a fitness class on Monday evenings. That left only Dad, who was slumped in front of the television after a day of DIY. Suddenly restless, Matt decided to go out while there was still daylight left. With Easter passed, the cool of the evening was full of summer's promise.

From habit, he looked down towards the car park in case Tig and Rob were loitering, but there was no sign of them. It hadn't been easy at school today; he had pointedly kept well away from them in all his lessons, apart from in maths, where Mr Bedwell wouldn't let people change places, and had sat with Bryn and James. Tig knew why. At break, he had sneered, 'Wimp! Hiding behind Hughesie's brother! You're not so hard when *he's* not around!' Matt only shrugged, with a throwaway 'Whatever', calculated to annoy. Tig would soon find someone else to pick on.

'Oy! Lank! Lanky Lanchester!'

Oh. There they were, lurking by the public toilet.

'Mank! Manky Lanchester!'

Robbo, hooting and capering; Tig, hands in pockets, looking at him with that half-smile that was now an open sneer.

'Skank! Skanky Lanchester—'

'Don't you ever get bored, hanging round public bogs?' Matt cut in. Without thinking, he'd stopped by the kerb, one foot on the pavement.

'You'd know all about bored, saddo,' Tig jeered. 'Riding round on your little bikie, all on your own.'

'Give it a rest, Tiggy-Winkle!' Matt fired back, before he'd even thought about it. It was handy for once, having a mum who was keen on old children's books.

Rob was delighted. 'Tiggy-Winkle! Tiggy-Winkle!' He grinned into Tig's face and gave him a shove; the joke was on Tig now.

Before Tig had time to retaliate, Matt left them to it, pushing off downhill to the junction and away.

From habit, he turned into Forest Road and up, pausing at the M.L. tree. Something had changed. For the first time Matt saw that its buds, at the ends of the twigs that divided and divided, were starting to open out into new leaves, ruddy-green, shiny moist, as if new-hatched and exposed to air for the first time. At the tree's base, someone had placed a fresh posy of cowslips, bunched and held by an elastic band.

Matt knew now who it was that left flowers for Martin. It was Wil.

Wil, picking small posies from his garden, of whatever flowers were in season. Wil, remembering.

But Matt knew that something had been resolved, up there on the hillside. He knew that Martin didn't need him any more.

'Sure?' he asked the tree.

No answer. Yes, he was sure. Martin was at peace and so, Matt hoped, was Wil, in the knowledge that he hadn't caused the accident.

Matt pushed on up the hill. Farther, a bit farther, the curve of the lane drew him on; one more bend, far enough to see Wil's cottage. He liked the way it was tucked in snug against its trees, its windows lit, a plume of smoke rising from the chimney.

There was one thing he still hadn't found out. Even though he hadn't meant to go to Wil's tonight, he left his bike on the verge, went up the path and knocked at the door. Inside, he heard Gwynnie stumping towards him with her stick; saw her look through the glass panel at the top of the door before opening it. There was no barking; that meant Jacko must be out with Wil.

'Matt! Hello – I didn't expect you today. Wil's not here – he and Jacko are helping Lewis up at the farm, with the lambs. Come on in, though.'

He followed her in, and sat on the cushiony stool she offered him.

'Is he all right now?'

She looked at him. 'In a way he is, and in a way he isn't.'

'Oh,' Matt said, unsure.

'I mean the way he's been getting things confused,' she said. 'Wandering in his mind – the way old people sometimes do. I've made an appointment with the doctor for next week. But I'm here now to look after him, and things'll be better. Anyway, you don't want to talk about dreary things like doctors and diseases, do you?'

'Actually I was going to ask you something,' Matt said.

'Oh?'

'About your story.'

Gwynnie looked blank; Matt tried again. 'That story you wrote. About Tommy Jones. I read it. I wasn't meant to. It was only a mistake it was there with the other books Will brought in. It's back here now, but anyway it was there in the box and I read it.'

'Wait a minute.' Gwynnie had been listening intently, puzzled. 'You're telling me Wil took one of my stories, one of my old bits of rubbish, down to your Mum's shop, along with all the proper books?'

Matt nodded; he'd thought she already knew.

Gwynnie's face cleared. 'I knew there was something! Something he was worried about! I see what must have happened. It would have been about the time I started having trouble with my hip, when I wrote that one, and instead of taking it upstairs – I've got a whole box full of them up there – I tucked it on the shelf, at one end. So you read my story, did you? My silly ramblings?' She looked pleased, though, rather than cross.

'It wasn't silly. It was good,' Matt told her. 'And I've been to the Tommy Jones place, I mean the obelisk, with Adam and the twins, and Ad lent me this other book, a version of the story, only

191

it wasn't nearly as good as yours.'

'Well!' Gwynnie sat back in her chair and looked at him as if he'd given her the most marvellous present. 'You didn't come all the way here to tell me that, though!'

'No,' Matt said. 'I wanted to ask you about Gwilym. The dog.'

'Oh! Gwilym.' Gwynnie smiled, and looked into the fire. 'Well. Gwilym was a dog we used to have, Wil and me. The first dog we had after we got married. We've had a few, since, but I'll always remember Gwilym. He wasn't a border collie like Jacko – more like a mongrel hound, a lurcher. Grey, rough-coated he was, taller than Jacko. Used to look after Owen, he did. Dear faithful Gwilym.' She gave a sigh that had a smile in it. 'The funny thing was, after he died – we had other dogs, like I said, but none of them quite like him – I used to imagine he was still here. I'd look out of the window from my bedroom, and think I saw him outside, guarding the house. And that's what happens when you write stories. You can't help adding little bits of yourself. I couldn't resist giving Tommy my Gwilym, for comfort. But really, if he'd had a Gwilym to look after him, I don't suppose he'd have got lost at all, poor little boy.'

'It was a sad story though – for Gwilym, I mean. He couldn't save Tommy.'

'Mm. The thing is, some endings you can change, and some you can't.'

Matt had the feeling that she wasn't only talking about Gwilym and Tommy Jones.

'We all have to look after each other,' Gwynnie said. 'That's what living's all about. I've got a photo of him somewhere – I'll look it out for you next time you come. Fancy you asking about him!'

Matt hesitated, then said: 'I think – I *saw* him, too. I think Gwilym was looking after Wil – you know, when he went off in the rain.'

Gwynnie didn't appear to find this as weird as most people would. 'Well, there are stranger things,' she said, looking at him very seriously.

Matt gave an embarrassed laugh. 'Anyway,' he went on. 'I think you ought to write more of those stories. You're good at it. And you ought to let people read them.'

She smiled. 'It's kind of you to say so. But there's one thing about living near Hay – you can't help thinking there are more than enough books in the world! I don't know. I only wrote them for myself.' Then she smiled at Matt. 'Still, you've read my story, and now it's there in *your* head – amazing, isn't it? I put marks on paper, and you looked at them, and that old story came to life again, and Tommy Jones and Gwilym with it! Almost a miracle when you think of it like that. Maybe I *will* have another go.'

'The twins are going to call their new puppy Gwilym,' Matt said. 'It was my idea.'

'A good one. It's a good name,' said Gwynnie. 'Anyway, shouldn't you be getting home now, before it gets dark?'

Matt said goodbye, and went out to his bike. 'Put your lights on, won't you, and be careful!' Gwynnie called after him. 'We don't want anyone else getting lost!'

Matt waved, and pushed off, freewheeling. Before turning right at the fork, something made him stop and glance back over his shoulder.

For an eye-blink, in the dusk, he thought he saw the grey shape of a dog by the cottage gate, watchful, guarding. But when he stopped the bike to turn round properly for a better look, there was nothing there at all.

Acknowledgements

Thank you to all the following people, who have helped me in large or small ways. To Jon Appleton, Adèle Geras, Jane Hughes, Linda Kempton, Linda Sargent, Christine Lo and of course Fiona Kennedy for editing and comments; to Gillian Fraser, Bethan Hughes, John Arwel Jones, Nia Jones, Graeme Sims and June Simmons for details of working dogs, second-hand bookselling and the Welsh language; to Bethan Hughes especially for giving me a nudge in this direction; and not least to Jess Meserve for her beautiful cover design.

Also by Linda Newbery

At the Firefly Gate

A haunting story of friendships
that stretch across the years.

"This beautifully written, atmospheric novel is cut from
the same character-centered cloth as such classic British
ghost stories as Philippa Pearce's *Tom's Midnight Garden* and
Lucy Boston's Children of Green Knowe books. . . .
A worthwhile addition to any collection."
—*Kirkus Reviews*

"With a strong sense of place, well-drawn characters, amusing
incidents, and an intriguing ghost story, [*At the Firefly Gate*]
has much appeal and many virtues."
—*The Horn Book Magazine*

"Quietly suspenseful. . . . An abundance of small satisfactions
await readers attuned to this novel's gentle cadences."
—*Publishers Weekly*

LINDA NEWBERY wanted to be an author from the age of about eight, but for a long time, everything she wrote stayed hidden in her wardrobe (where some of it can still be found). It wasn't until many years later that she began submitting her work to publishers. She has written more than twenty books for children and young adults, including *At the Firefly Gate, Sisterland, The Shell House,* and *Set in Stone,* which won the prestigious Costa Award (formerly the Whitbread Prize) for Children's Book of the Year.

Linda enjoys writing short stories and poetry as well as novels and is a regular teacher of writing courses for children, teenagers, and adults. She lives in Northamptonshire with her husband and three cats.